A CHANGE IN PLANS

"Now what?" Neely said as soon as Boone was gone.

Mitch put his finger to his lips. He walked over to the door and looked out. When he'd made sure that Boone wasn't hanging around outside, he said, "After what he said, we might have to change our plans."

"I knew we couldn't keep taking Cady's men out one at a time," Neely said. "They were bound to catch on."

"They haven't caught on yet," Mitch told him. "I don't think they know what's happening. They're just suspicious."

"They killed Gooden," Neely pointed out. "That means they're more than suspicious. They're dangerous."

"We knew that already," Riley said. "Gooden wasn't the first one they killed."

"Yeah," Neely said. "But what are we gonna do about it?"

"We might have to change our plans," Mitch said.

"How?"

"We might have to try to get them all at once."

Apache Law

Outlaw Town

Luke Adams

LEISURE BOOKS NEW YORK CITY

A LEISURE BOOK®

June 2000

Published by

Dorchester Publishing Co., Inc.
276 Fifth Avenue
New York, NY 10001

ISBN 0-8439-4732-2

The name "Leisure Books" and the stylized "L" with design are trademarks of Dorchester Publishing Co., Inc.

Printed in the United States of America.

Outlaw Town

Chapter One

Three weeks after the itinerant evangelist named Deuce Davis left the booming mining town of Paxton, Bill Carson killed his wife, cleaned out the safe at J. Paxton Reid's mining shack, and took off over the mountain. It was the second time in as many months that Reid's safe had been robbed. Naturally, Reid wasn't too happy about it.

"I'm not saying I blame him for killing his wife," Reid told Mitch Frye. "She's probably better off. But the son of a bitch shouldn't have robbed me."

Mitch was Paxton's sheriff, though not by his own choice. He'd spent most of his life outside of towns, and he would have preferred living somewhere less crowded. But he'd been more or less tricked into taking the sheriff's job by Reid, who was the town's founder, mayor, and richest man.

"She was awful sick," Mitch said of Carson's wife. "Had been for a long time, from what I understand. I guess he just wanted to put a stop to her suffering."

"He's a murderer just the same," Reid said. "In the eyes of the law, that is."

Reid was a stout man with a red face and thinning hair. Frye tolerated him, but he didn't really like him or trust him, and for good reason.

"And he didn't have to rob me," Reid continued, coming to the part that Mitch figured he really cared about. "That just makes it worse."

"He must have killed her before he thought about what he was going to do afterward," Mitch said.

Reid had sent for him after he'd found his empty safe, and the two of them had gone to Carson's house. Mrs. Carson was laid out on the bed in her nightgown, her hands crossed on her chest. She'd been shot right through the heart. Mitch thought she might even have asked her husband to kill her, if she'd been suffering bad enough and long enough. There was almost the trace of a smile on her face, as if she'd died happy. Mitch and Reid had made arrangements for her burial before returning to Mitch's office.

"He should have thought things out," Reid said. "Hell, everyone in town knew his wife was sick. If he'd said something to me about why he did it, I might not even have had you arrest him."

Mitch's mouth twitched. He didn't like having Reid think that he could tell Mitch whom to arrest or not arrest. Reid might have put Mitch in the job, but as long as he was the sheriff, Mitch was going to do things as he saw fit.

"It was bad enough when Duncklee cleaned me out," Reid continued. "But at least you got that money back for me."

"I got your horses, too," Mitch said.

Hunting down Duncklee was what had led to Reid's offer to make Mitch sheriff of Paxton. Mitch had tried to turn down the job, but he'd made the mistake of signing a paper saying that he had tracked Duncklee down and killed him. The signature was just for the record, Reid had told him, but that hadn't been exactly true. Reid had threatened to use the paper as Frye's "confession" to murder if Frye refused to stay on as the law in Paxton.

"Yes, you got the horses back," Reid said. "I haven't forgotten. Now I want you to go after Carson."

"I didn't think you wanted me to leave town."

Reid gave Mitch a speculative look. "I think you'll come back. I trust you."

"You trusted Carson, too."

Carson was Reid's manager, or he had been up until the robbery. He had overseen all Reid's mining operations.

"I know I did," Reid said. "That was a mistake. But in your case, I don't think I have to worry."

Frye knew it wasn't trust alone that gave Reid his confidence. It was the paper Frye had signed. And there was something else besides, though Frye didn't really like to admit it, even to himself.

The something else was Reid's daughter, Jewel, who was unlike any woman Mitch had ever met. It didn't seem to bother her that Mitch was half Apache, though that was something that bothered a lot of folks Mitch had met in the course of his life. But Jewel had never even mentioned it. She was strong-minded and independent, too, not one bit afraid to stand up to her father, who wasn't too pleased that his daughter had taken up with Mitch.

9

"When do you want me to leave?" Mitch asked.

"Right now. I don't want that son of a bitch to get away."

It wasn't as if Reid was ordering him, Mitch told himself. Carson had killed his wife, after all, and he'd cleaned out Reid's safe. It was Mitch's job to do something about that.

"I'll have to let Alky know I'm leaving," Mitch said.

Alky was Mitch's deputy. Mitch had met him during the course of an investigation into a series of gruesome murders, and Alky had proved so helpful that Mitch had persuaded Reid to hire him.

"Where is he?" Reid asked.

"Probably over at the Eat Here. He likes a late breakfast."

"I'll tell him, then," Reid said. "I was going by there, myself."

Mitch suspected that Reid was more interested in Ellie West, who owned the Eat Here, than he was in food. He'd noticed the way the two of them looked at each other when they thought no one was watching.

"All right," Mitch said. "I'll get started right now."

Mitch kept his horse at Sam Neely's livery stable, which also served as Paxton's blacksmith shop. Neely was forking hay into a stall when Mitch walked in, and the dry, dusty smell of it filled the sheriff's nostrils. Mitch liked the smell. The town of Paxton was up on the side of a mountain, and hay wasn't easy to come by.

"Hey, Sheriff," Neely said. "I hear we've got trouble in town."

He walked over and stood near Mitch, stabbing the tines of the pitchfork into the dirt floor and leaning on the handle.

"You heard wrong," Mitch said. "The trouble's left already. Did Bill Carson stable his horse here?"

"I figured you'd be asking me that. He did, and he left here not long after daylight this morning."

"I don't guess you asked where he was going."

"Nope. Where a man goes isn't any of my business. I just stable the horses."

"And he didn't happen to say."

Neely grinned. "Matter of fact, he did. Said he'd been having a hard time lately, so he thought he'd just go for a little ride. I asked how his wife was feeling, and he said she was doing just fine now. I thought he meant she was feeling better till somebody came by and told me different."

"Which direction did he go?" Mitch asked.

"I knew you were going to ask me that, too. And I can tell you the answer. I walked out behind him as he left, to get myself a breath of fresh air, and he was headed on up the mountain."

There was only one road up the mountain into Paxton, and it continued through the town and up to the mines. After the last mine, the road just petered out into the scrub. As far as Mitch knew, no one had ever tried to get out of town by going over the mountain, though it could probably be done if a man was determined enough. Carson had plenty of reason to be determined.

"Was he carrying anything with him?" Mitch asked.

"Not that I noticed," Neely said.

That was why Carson had gone on up the mountain, Mitch thought. He hadn't opened the safe at the mining shack yet. He'd made a stop there before he left town. Mitch asked if Neely had seen Carson come back down.

"Nope. 'Course, it would be easy for me to miss him if I was busy and not looking out the door."

"All right. Go ahead and saddle my horse for me. I'm going after Carson."

Neely didn't move. "Bill's a good man," he said. "I know he killed his wife, but she was suffering mightily. It may be that she just couldn't stand any more of it."

"May be," Mitch agreed. "But Bill cleaned out Mr. Reid's safe. I have to bring him back. And the money, too."

"If I know Reid, he don't give a damn about whether you bring Bill back or not, long's he gets his money."

"I expect you're right about that," Mitch said.

It didn't take long after he reached Reid's mine for Mitch to locate Carson's trail. For a long time, he'd worked as a civilian scout for the Sixth Cavalry under the command of General Crook. It had been a job that suited Mitch perfectly, but General Phil Sheridan eventually decided that Crook's Apache and civilian scouts were never going to be able to keep Geronimo on the reservation. The scouts were all let go, and Mitch was on his own. He'd thought about the possibility of becoming a bounty hunter, but he'd decided against it until he'd become one more or less by accident. That had led him to his current employment, which was a far cry from tracking Apaches in the desert. But now and then those tracking skills came in handy.

Carson hadn't returned to town. He'd left the mining shack and ridden right on up the mountain. Mitch had been afraid that was the case. In a way, though, it might make things easier. There wasn't likely to be anyone else up there to interfere with Mitch's pursuit.

Mitch had picked up some supplies in town, just in case he had to go on up, so there was no reason for him to linger at the mine. He wished he'd had a chance to tell Jewel where he was going, but maybe Reid would do that.

On the other hand, maybe he wouldn't. He was just ornery enough not to, Mitch thought. He might think that Jewel would hold it against Mitch for not having told her he was leaving.

And she might. Or she might not even care, one way or the other. Mitch wasn't really sure exactly how their relationship stood. Certainly it had never gone beyond friendship, and even that word was a hard one for Mitch to use. Before now, his only real friends had been scouts like Tom Horn and Al Sieber, rough men like himself who understood a lot more about the ways of the Apache warriors than they did about women.

Thinking about Jewel and how he felt about her made Mitch uncomfortable. He kneed his horse and started after Bill Carson.

It took him three days to catch up with Carson, who'd proved a little trickier than Mitch would have thought. It was just after dark, and Carson had already set up for the night. He was squatted down by a low fire boiling coffee when Mitch walked into his camp.

Carson hardly bothered to look up. "I thought I'd be seeing you before long. I've felt you at my back for a day or so now."

"It shouldn't have taken me so long," Mitch said. He was holding his Colt's Peacemaker in his right hand, pointing it at Carson. "I must be slipping."

"You've just been living in town too long. You want some of this coffee?"

Mitch nodded. "It'd taste pretty good. I have a cup in my saddlebags."

He reached into the saddlebags with his left hand and rummaged around until he found the tin cup, never taking his eyes off Carson. He tossed the cup over by the fire.

Carson took the cup and set it upright. Then he poured it full of coffee.

"You could just shoot me now," he said. "Then you could have your coffee without having to worry about me."

"I'll let it cool for a little while," Mitch told him.

Carson poured some coffee into his own cup. "I like mine hot," he said, and drank.

"Why'd you kill her?" Mitch asked.

Carson looked at him over the rim of the cup. "She was hurting all the time. She knew she was never going to get better, and so did I. She could have stood it, I reckon. But I couldn't. I couldn't stand to see her like that anymore."

Mitch nodded. That was about the way he'd figured it. "What about the money? Why'd you take that?"

"I needed a stake. I'd saved up a little from what Reid paid me, but not enough to make much of a start on."

"You could've stayed in Paxton. It might be that people would've understood why you did what you did."

Carson took another sip of his coffee, swallowed, and said, "Maybe, maybe not. I never thought about it that much. Looking at her there on that bed, peaceful for the first time in a couple of weeks, I knew I'd done the right thing. But I didn't expect anybody else to see it that way."

"I guess not," Mitch said. "Now that you've thought it over, though, you might see things a little different. You can come back with me, give Reid his money back, and take your chances with the town. Things'll probably work out all right for you."

"Or they might not," Carson said. "Fella never can tell about things like that."

"That's right. But it's worth a chance."

Carson looked into the fire and didn't say anything. Neither did Mitch. A couple of minutes went by, and Carson looked up.

"You going to drink any of this coffee or not?" Carson asked, indicating Mitch's cup with his own.

"I might as well," Mitch said.

He dropped his horse's reins, knowing the animal would stay put, and walked over to where Carson squatted by the fire.

"Kind of an interesting situation, ain't it," Carson said. "You know that coffee'll taste mighty good after a day in the saddle, but you can't be sure I won't try something now that I've got you over here."

"Oh, I'm pretty sure about that," Mitch said.

And he was. He knew that Carson had made his decision while he was looking into the fire, which meant that Mitch was ready when Carson sprang up and threw hot coffee right at his face.

Mitch stepped aside and most of the coffee missed him, though a few drops did stain the arm of his shirt. Carson dropped the cup and started to go for his pistol. Even when he saw that it wouldn't do any good, even when he must have known it was a futile effort, he kept on with his play.

Mitch waited until Carson's pistol had cleared the holster. At that point, he didn't have any choice. He fired his pistol.

Carson was jolted backward for a step or two. Then he looked at Mitch and opened his mouth as if he had something to say.

Whatever it was, he never got it out. His knees gave way, and he toppled forward to fall facedown at the edge of the campfire.

Mitch holstered his pistol and bent down to move Carson away from the fire before it singed his hair. Mitch had never liked the smell of burning hair. He turned Carson over and closed his eyes. Then he looked for his coffee cup.

It was sitting right where Carson had set it, still upright, still full of coffee. Mitch squatted down and picked it up. Then he took a sip. It was just the way he liked it. Not too hot, but not yet cool. It didn't taste as good as he'd thought it would, however. Carson had been a good man. Mitch had liked him. He poured the coffee on the ground.

"Goddamn it," he said.

Chapter Two

Mitch buried Carson near the camp. He stacked stones on the grave to keep the animals from scattering the bones, and he never even considered taking Carson's head back to prove to Reid that his mine manager was dead. He'd taken Duncklee's head, but that had been different. If Reid wanted to think Carson was still alive, that was fine with Mitch.

The money that Carson had stolen was in his saddlebags. Mitch left it there, since he was going to take Carson's horse back. He could sell the horse and tack to Neely. Carson's rifle and pistol Mitch would keep in his office. You never knew when you might need an extra gun.

The return trip to Paxton didn't take long, since Mitch could stick to the roads, something that Carson hadn't done. And now that he wasn't tracking anyone, Mitch could travel at his own speed.

There was only one problem.

He wasn't going to be allowed to return to Paxton.

It was late the next afternoon when he arrived at a point about three quarters of the way up the road leading to town and was stopped by a man with a Winchester.

The man got up from where he'd been sitting beside a large rock and stepped out in the middle of the trail in front of Mitch, holding the rifle casually in one hand. He was tall and wide and had a thick black beard. He didn't look the least bit friendly. Mitch had never seen him before.

"You can hold it right there," he told Mitch.

Mitch reined in his horse and said, "What's the trouble?"

"No trouble. Not your trouble, anyhow. It's just that you'll have to turn back. Paxton's under quarantine."

"Quarantine?" Mitch said, wondering what the hell was going on. Pretty much everybody in town had been perfectly healthy when he left.

"That's right," the stranger said. Mitch could hardly see his mouth in the thicket of beard. "Quarantine. Nobody gets, in, nobody gets out. You'd best turn around and go right on back where you came from."

"I'm willing to take my chances," Mitch said, starting his horse forward.

The stranger took a step back and raised his rifle. He aimed it at somewhere around the middle of Mitch's chest.

"You might be willing, but I'm not," the man said. "One way or the other, this is as far as you go."

Mitch pulled lightly on the reins, and his horse stopped. There had to be an explanation for what was happening, but if there was, Mitch couldn't figure it. One thing was for sure, though: The man with the rifle looked damned determined not to let him pass.

"All right," Mitch said. "I'm turning back. But I have business up in the town."

The rifle didn't waver. "Be a good idea for you to take your business somewhere else. No telling when things'll run their course here."

Mitch didn't say anything to that. He turned his horse and started it walking slowly back down the road, leading Carson's horse along behind. Just before he rounded the first curve, he looked back. The man with the rifle was still standing there, still alert.

That was fine with Mitch, who had decided almost the instant he'd seen the man that something was very wrong, all right. But Mitch was sure it wasn't anything that required a quarantine. It was something different. And it might even be something worse.

Whatever it was, Mitch was going to find out.

He rode until he came to a wide place in the road where a man could make camp if he was of a mind to. Mitch didn't think it would be a good idea to camp out in the open, however, so he rode on into the trees until he found a spot that was out of sight of the road and not too far from the little stream that ran down the mountainside.

The first thing he did was take the saddlebags off Carson's horse and hide Reid's money. He gave some grain to both horses and led them to the stream and let them drink. By that time it was getting dark. He staked the horses, ate some cold beans out of a can, and thought about what he was going to do.

It seemed to him that the best idea would be to slip into town unnoticed. He didn't think it would be hard to do. There'd most likely be someone guarding the road even at night, but Mitch didn't need the road.

He also figured that he'd better be careful. He hadn't been wearing a badge, mainly because he didn't have one. So the stranger didn't know who he was. For all the stranger knew, Mitch could have been someone riding up to try his luck at mining, maybe to stake a claim. There was no reason for him to suspect that Mitch was the law, which Mitch figured was a good thing. The stranger didn't look like a man who would get along well with the law.

Mitch waited until well after nightfall to start back toward the town. The only sounds were the ripple of the stream and the whisper of the poplar leaves in the slight breeze. Mitch himself made no noise at all.

He had little trouble getting up the mountain. The moon gave plenty of light, and all Mitch had to do was follow the stream, which trickled down from the mines and ran just in back of the town.

During the daylight hours, Paxton was generally a bustling community. People and wagons were on the street, the saloons were open, and the stores did a lively business.

The place was usually fairly active at night, too. The miners often had plenty of money to spend, so the saloons, some of which were set up in tents, really got going about dark, and business in the whorehouses picked up considerably.

But the town was strangely silent when Mitch arrived in back of the Bad Dog Saloon, one of the few saloons in town that was in an actual building.

The saloon itself seemed to be lively enough. The place was lit up, and Mitch could hear music from inside it. Mitch stood in the shadows and listened for a minute while he looked out at the street.

There was hardly anyone around. At that time of night there should have been people coming and going from one place or another, but there was no movement. And the Golden Monkey, a tent saloon down the street, was dark and quiet.

Another thing that bothered Mitch was that while there were at least a few people out and about, he didn't recognize a single one of them. And he didn't like it that they weren't moving from place to place. They were standing around all too casually, as if keeping watch.

Something was very wrong, all right.

Staying in the shadows and keeping well out of sight of the men along the street, Mitch made his way to his office. After making sure no one was watching, he slipped through the unlocked door and went inside. There was no one there. The big oak desk sat in the middle of the room, papers strewn across the top. The gun cabinet was locked, the guns still inside, but there was no sign of Alky.

Next Mitch went to the jail, still taking care not to be seen. There was no one in the jail, either. The cells were empty and silent. Usually there was at least one occupied cell. Hardly a night passed in a boomtown like Paxton without someone getting drunk and starting a fight that ended only when Mitch or Alky broke it up and hauled the worst offenders off to the jail to sleep off their whiskey-induced belligerence.

Not tonight.

Mitch sat on one of the cots and looked out the barred window at the night sky and the stars. There weren't any answers there.

He figured the answers he was looking for were at the Bad Dog, but when he thought about the man on the trail, he had an idea he wouldn't be received with any great hospitality if he went to the saloon.

He could go up to one of the mines, but he wasn't sure how he'd be received there, either. If there was something bad going on in the town, the miners might be more inclined to shoot than to talk.

So he decided to go to Fanny Belle's whorehouse, though *house* was the wrong word, considering that the operation was housed in a big tent.

He got almost to Fanny Belle's without incident. Then he got careless.

It was something he would never have done in the days when he'd been chasing Geronimo, but living in town had had an effect on him, maybe more of an effect than he'd realized. Carson had joked about it, but it was true.

To get to Fanny Belle's, he had to cross the street, which meant that he would be exposed in the moonlight for a brief moment. In the old days, not really that long ago, he would have waited for a cloud, or he would have looked more closely into the shadows of the buildings.

But now he gave a cursory glance, didn't see anyone, and hotfooted it across the dusty street.

Mitch was almost at the entrance of Fanny Belle's tent when someone stepped out of the darkness at the side of the tent and jammed a pistol barrel into his ribs, hard enough to bruise him.

Mitch had been surprised a time or two in his life. Anyone who tries to outsmart Apaches was bound to have been fooled more than once. But what made Mitch angry this time was that he'd walked right into it, knowing better all the time.

But the man who had the pistol had made a mistake,

too, and his was a lot worse than Mitch's. He'd gotten much too close to a very dangerous man without knowing whom he was bracing.

It was a mistake that he wouldn't be making again anytime soon.

Mitch swept his left hand up, shoving the pistol aside. At almost the same instant he stomped on the man's instep as hard as he could. When the man opened his mouth to yell, Mitch smashed his right hand into the man's jaw, clapping his mouth shut with an audible click. As the man started to fold, Mitch whipped out his own pistol and cracked it hard against the side of his head.

The man went down and didn't move. The whole thing happened in only a couple of seconds, and no one had made a noise loud enough to attract any attention at a distance of more than ten feet. Mitch dragged the man into the shadows, took his pistol, and left him lying there. Then he went into Fanny Belle's tent.

The only person there was Fanny Belle herself. Not a single one of her girls was around, and there were no customers. Fanny Belle was sitting at a little table drinking whiskey from a tumbler, which was nothing unusual. Mitch couldn't remember having seen her without a drink in her hand or nearby.

"Evening, Sheriff," she said when she saw him. "How about a drink?"

"Not right now," Mitch said. "What the hell's going on around here, Fanny Belle?"

"You'd better have a seat, Sheriff. And stay out of sight. How'd you get in here, anyway? There's a man outside watching the place."

"Not now," Mitch said.

Fanny Belle took a drink, then said, "Oh. Well, I'm glad to hear it. Sure you don't want a drink? You're looking pretty rough."

Mitch hadn't shaved while he'd been on the trail. To tell the truth, he hadn't had a bath, either. And his clothes were dirty with trail dust.

"No."

"I do."

She poured her glass full from a bottle that sat on the table and took a swallow.

"Make you feel better?" Mitch asked.

Fanny Belle smiled. "Sometimes."

"Good. Now tell me what's happening here. Why is there a man guarding your door? Where is everybody? What's going on in the Bad Dog?"

"You're full of questions, ain't you? You shouldn't have stayed gone for so long. If you'd been here, you'd know what's happening."

"I was only gone for four days."

"Lot can happen in four days."

"I guess it can." Mitch watched her take a swallow of her drink. "And I guess I can use some of that whiskey now."

Fanny Belle got up and found another glass. She brought it back to the table and poured Mitch's drink.

He took a swallow and enjoyed the burn. Now and then, maybe once a year, Mitch really tied one on, but this wasn't the time. Just a little drink to settle him. That's all he needed.

Fanny Belle needed a lot more than that, but it never seemed to touch her. Her speech never slurred, her eyes never dimmed.

"Good stuff," Mitch said.

"My own bottle. I wouldn't sell any of it to the customers."

"Don't blame you." Mitch set his glass on the table. "Now tell me about what happened."

"Well," Fanny Belle said, "it all started the day after you left. That's when Rance Cady and his men rode into town."

Mitch had heard of Rance Cady. He and his gang were wanted in three or four states. They'd robbed a train or two and a couple of banks. Killed five men that Mitch knew of, and probably more.

"It wasn't so bad to start with," Fanny Belle said. "They just about took over the town, but they weren't any worse than a lot of folks. Lots of drinking and helling around. Shooting and carousing. Came in here and took over. That's when things started getting a little ugly. They didn't want to pay. One of them started hitting Rainbow."

Mitch knew Rainbow, too. "What did you do about that?"

"Not a thing. Your deputy came in about then. He's a runty little fella, but he ain't afraid of a damn thing. He made them stop."

Mitch wasn't surprised. "Where's Alky now?"

"Over at the Bad Dog, I expect. That's where Cady's got all of them."

"All of who?"

"His hostages," Fanny Belle said. "That's what Rance Cady's done. He's taken the whole damn town hostage."

Mitch thought about what she was telling him. It didn't seem likely. It didn't even seem possible.

"He doesn't have you," Mitch pointed out.

"He might as well have." Fanny Belle took a long swallow of whiskey. A tear leaked out of one eye. "He's got Rainbow. He said he'd kill her if I did anything to bother him."

Mitch hadn't known Fanny Belle cared for Rainbow that way.

"That's what he did, see," Fanny Belle said. "He couldn't take everybody, but he took someone that nearly everybody cared about. He'll kill them all if we don't do what he says."

"Jewel," Mitch said.

"Her, George Kelley, Reid, Red Collins, he's got 'em all."

Kelley was the banker, and Collins was the owner of the Bad Dog. Mitch assumed that by *all* Belle meant most of the town's prominent citizens.

"Why?" he said.

Fanny Belle finished her whiskey and set the glass down on the table. "Money. He says he'll leave when he has enough."

"Why didn't he just rob the bank?"

"Hell, he didn't have to. He made Kelley give him the money, but it wasn't enough to satisfy him. Not when he'd thought things over."

Fanny Belle refilled her glass and held the bottle up to Mitch, half of whose drink was still untasted.

"See," Fanny Belle said, "Cady decided that he didn't have to settle for just what he could get out of the bank. He decided he could have more."

"How much more does he want?" Mitch asked.

Fanny Belle sighed. "He wants it all."

Chapter Three

Rance Cady was having a fine time in the Bad Dog Saloon. The whiskey was free, the piano man would play anything Cady asked for, and the women were all more than willing to share their charms with him. Or, hell, maybe they weren't all that willing, but they didn't dare let on to him about it. It hadn't taken Cady long to realize that he really liked having a saloon all his own, and he wondered why he'd never thought of taking one over before.

Probably it was because he'd never found a town quite like Paxton before, he decided. That had to be it. Where else could you find an isolated mining town, with one road in and the same road out? Not many places, Cady was sure. But what a perfect situation Paxton was for someone with guts and guns (and Cady had plenty of both) to step in and set himself up as the one man who controlled everything.

He hadn't planned it that way from the beginning, he

had to admit. He'd more or less stumbled onto the town while looking for a place to stay out of the way of the law for a while. He hadn't really thought much beyond that until he thought about the town and its situation for a day or so. Then the plan had begun to take shape.

At first he'd thought he could just clean out the bank and maybe a couple of the saloons, but then he'd had his great idea. Why settle for a part when he could have the whole? Never let it be said that Rance Cady passed up the chance to become a very rich man.

He talked it over with Gil Boone while they were drinking whiskey in the Bad Dog.

"I don't get it," Gil said after Rance had explained things to him.

Gil Boone was a big, sloppy man, completely bald, with jowls that drooped down and made him appear to wear a perpetual frown. He wasn't exactly smart, but he had two great assets, at least as far as Cady was concerned: He didn't have any semblance of a conscience, and he was absolutely loyal to Cady.

"It's simple," Cady said, taking the time to say everything slowly and clearly, in short sentences. "We take over the town. Make the whole place ours. Make them work the mines for us."

Boone rolled a cigarette and lit it. After he'd thought it over in his slow way, he said, "Sounds like you're thinking of settling. I never took to the idea of staying in one place too long."

"We wouldn't stay too long," Cady assured him. "Just long enough to get so much gold that we could head on down to Mexico and never have to worry about money again."

Boone narrowed his eyes against the smoke that was hanging in front of his face. "When you put it that way, it makes sense. I don't see how you think you can take over a whole town, though."

"It's going to be easy," Cady said, and then he told Boone all about how they were going to do it.

"So that's what they did," Fanny Belle said, finishing her version of the story to Mitch. "They rounded up everyone they could think of, took them to the Bad Dog, and locked the doors. Nobody gets in or out without Cady's say-so. He says he'll kill all of them if we don't do what he tells us."

"Didn't anyone put up a fight?" Mitch asked.

"Sure they did. That deputy of yours, for one. But Cady just started shooting people. That took the fight out of everyone pretty quick."

"Who did he kill?"

"One of Red Collins's girls was the first. Red didn't take kindly to Cady making his headquarters in the Bad Dog, and he and that deputy tried to stop him. But Cady shut them up quick when he shot that girl. Showed he meant business. Nobody wanted to put up much of a fight after that."

"But there are still plenty of men up in the mines and in town. Enough to take Cady and his gang."

"Sure there are. But do you want Cady to kill your friend Miss Reid? And her daddy? And Rainbow, and—"

"Never mind," Mitch said. "I see where're you're going."

"Besides," Fanny Belle said, looking at her empty glass and reaching for the whiskey bottle. "Cady's not

29

taking from everybody. Just from the biggest. He wants two weeks' worth of gold from Reid's mine, from Taylor's, from Gooden's, and from Nolan's. Everybody else can go ahead and work his own mine, and Cady won't bother 'em."

"I guess Cady has Sam Taylor, Harp Gooden, and Jesse Nolan in the Bad Dog," Mitch said.

"That's right, and you can bet they told their men to do whatever Cady said. They want to get out of this alive."

"There's one thing Cady doesn't know about, though," Mitch said.

"What's that?" Fanny Belle wanted to know.

"He doesn't know about me."

"He will, though," Fanny Belle said. "Soon as that fella you coldcocked out there gets around to telling him."

Mitch had forgotten about the man who'd stopped him outside Fanny Belle's tent.

"Unless you killed him, that is," Fanny Belle said hopefully.

"I didn't," Mitch said, though he wasn't really sure. He'd hit the man pretty hard, it depended on how hard his head happened to be.

Fanny Belle shook her head sadly. "Too bad you didn't finish him."

"It's not too late," Mitch said.

Fanny Belle looked at him across the table. "It's none of my business, but I'd just as soon you went out there and did the job."

"What will Cady do when one of his men is missing?"

"Hell, he won't do much. What can he do if he don't know what happened? A man might decide to ride down the mountain and out of here, for all Cady knows."

He'd have to pass the sentry, though, Mitch thought. *But sentries have been known to sleep at their posts.*

"How many men does Cady have?" he asked.

"Around twenty, give or take."

Mitch wondered how many of them he could dispose of before Cady figured out that something was going on. He'd have to be careful. He didn't want Cady to start killing off his hostages.

"You gonna do it?"

"Do what?" Mitch asked.

"You gonna kill him?"

"I might. It's what comes next that I'm thinking about."

"I'll help," Fanny Belle said. "Cady lets his men come here now and then, during the day. They're the only ones he lets on the streets at night, so they can't come then. But when they do, I can find out things. I can even kill a few of them for you."

"You don't have to kill anybody," Mitch said. "Not yet."

"I wouldn't mind."

He was sure she wouldn't.

"Let me see what I can do first. Does Cady have Ellie West in the Bad Dog?"

"No. He wanted her out so she could cook. But if you're thinking about having her put poison in the food, you can forget it."

It was as if Fanny Belle had been reading Mitch's mind, which made him feel a little uncomfortable.

"Why?" he asked.

"Because not everybody in Cady's gang eats at once. And he'll kill Reid if any one of 'em gets sick. Ellie wouldn't like that."

Mitch had always thought there was something going

on between Reid and Ellie West, but he hadn't been sure. He wondered how Cady had figured it out so soon, not that it mattered.

"So what're you gonna do?" Fanny Belle asked.

"I'll think of something," Mitch said.

Fanny Belle gave him a speculative look. "I'll just bet you will," she said.

Chapter Four

Mitch went outside. The man he'd hit was still lying where Mitch had left him, breathing raggedly through his mouth. No one had come to check on him, but Mitch knew he couldn't be left there even if he was dead. Mitch had to hide the body.

It took him a few minutes, but Mitch managed to get the man on his feet and maneuver him through the alley in back of Belle's tent and head him in the direction of Sam Neely's livery stable.

By the time they got almost to the stable, the man was waking up. Mitch didn't think he was going to be able to get him inside quietly, so he pulled out his pistol and hit him in the head again. Hard.

The man sagged to the ground without making a sound. Mitch checked the street, saw no one around, then dragged him the rest of the way to Neely's.

Mitch had no way of knowing whether Neely was in

the Bad Dog. He wished he'd asked Fanny Belle, but he hadn't thought of it. He dropped the man in the shadows and went to check the stable.

The doors to the livery were shut but not locked. Mitch pushed them open slightly. There was no light inside and no sign of Neely. Mitch went back for the man he'd left in the dirt.

When Mitch bent down, he noticed that the man wasn't breathing.

I guess I hit him a little too hard that time, Mitch thought. It was just as well. He dragged the man inside. It was very dark. Mitch dragged the man to the back and propped him against the wall of an empty stall.

When he stepped out of the stall, Sam Neely was standing there, pointing a shotgun at him.

"Who the hell are you, and what are you doing here?" Neely said.

"It's me, Sam," Mitch said.

"Sheriff? I didn't recognize you in the dark. What's going on?"

"I was leaving you someone to take care of. Except that he doesn't need taking care of anymore."

"Good. I like taking care of horses, but I don't give much of a damn for people. 'Specially not the ones around here these days."

"I'm going to try to do something about that," Mitch said.

"That won't be easy. There's a damn big bunch of them."

"So I've heard. But there's one less than there was a little while ago." Mitch hooked a thumb in the direction of the stall. "What's left of him is back there."

"Then I'll have to take care of him, one way or the other. Don't want him stinking up the place. But that's all right. I'd rather deal with him dead than alive."

"I'll help you," Mitch said.

"Don't worry about it. How'd you get back here to town, anyway?"

Mitch told him.

"Yeah, it'd be easy enough to get by the fella they've got down there on the road if you wanted to. It's just that not many people would want to get to Paxton bad enough to take off through the trees. Cady's got us pretty well tied up."

"I'll see what I can do about it. Can I stay here tonight?"

"Fine with me. What about tomorrow?"

The way Mitch had it figured, he could walk the streets freely during the day. He didn't look much like a sheriff; in fact, he looked like a miner, and there was no way Cady or his men could keep up with everyone who belonged in Paxton. As far as they were concerned, he was just another man who'd been there all along. As long as he didn't cause them any trouble, they wouldn't bother him.

There was just one problem. If any of the town's citizens slipped up and acknowledged him as the sheriff, he was going to be in big trouble.

Well, that was just something he'd have to work out as he went along.

"I'll worry about tomorrow when the sun comes up," he said. "Right now, what I'd like to do is have a look around the town and then come back here and get some sleep."

"Be careful," Neely said.

"Don't worry," Mitch said. "I will."

The Bad Dog Saloon was not noted for its windows. There were two, but they weren't large, and both of them faced the street. There was no way for Mitch to get a look inside through them, because a couple of Cady's men were lounging close by. To Mitch, who was observing them from the dark shadows of the alley, they seemed to be alert and ready for trouble in spite of their casual attitudes. Cady would have some of his best men out there. He wouldn't want anyone slipping up on him.

But there were other ways to see what was going on in the Bad Dog. The building was a rambling one-story structure with rooms on the back where Red Collins's girls could earn a little money for themselves, and for Red. If Mitch could get into one of the rooms, he might be able to find out a little bit about what was going on and how Jewel and the others were being treated.

Getting into the rooms would be tricky, however, if Cady had thought to have someone guard the back of the building, and there was no reason to think he hadn't. The back was even more vulnerable than the front, and Cady had two men out there.

Mitch slipped along between two buildings until he came to the alley in back of the Bad Dog. It was as quiet and dark as the bottom of one of the Paxton mines. Smells of garbage and dust were in the air.

Nothing moved in the alley, but Mitch was in no hurry. He knew at least as much about being still and quiet as any man that Rance Cady had, and probably more. His years as a scout had taught him the value of stillness, and he thought that patience was probably bred into his bones. When it came to quiet watching, the Apache couldn't be outdone.

So Mitch found a particularly dark spot beside a wooden rain barrel and settled down to wait.

He didn't know how long he waited. Counting the minutes was always a mistake. It didn't do to think too much, either. Thinking was a distraction. The best way to wait was to make your mind a receptive blank, letting it receive all the impressions of the night: the smells, the sounds, the silences, the movements.

All the sounds were coming from the Bad Dog. The laughter was loud, and Mitch figured most of it was being done by Cady and his men, the ones who weren't out patrolling the town or watching the building. The piano didn't sound any different from usual. It was always a little out of tune.

There were no lights in the back rooms. Either no one was there, or whoever was there preferred to take pleasure in the dark.

After Mitch had been squatting beside the rain barrel for a good while, there was a ripple in a shadow near the back wall of the Bad Dog. A bit of darkness moved outward and became the figure of a man who must have been leaning against the wall. He looked up and down the alley. Seeing no one, he stretched and rolled a cigarette. When he lit it, Mitch could see a little of his face, but not enough so that he would recognize him if he saw him again.

The man flipped the match away, and it made a short red arc before it burned out and fell to the ground. After a second, Mitch could smell the smoke from the cigarette. Smoking was a careless thing to do, and it showed that Cady's man didn't really expect anyone to be out there in the alley with him.

But careless as he may have been, the man didn't leave his post. He was better disciplined than Mitch had expected. After he'd smoked for a short time, he faded back into the night, the glowing tip of the cigarette and the smell of smoke the only things left to indicate that he'd been there at all. Soon the tip dropped to the ground and disappeared.

Mitch wasn't going to be able to get inside the Bad Dog through the rear, not unless he did something about the guard, and he wasn't ready for that. One of Cady's men had already disappeared, and if something were to happen to another one, Cady would almost certainly become suspicious and begin to take his worries out on his hostages. Mitch didn't want that to happen.

So he faded silently away into the night.

Rance Cady, on the other hand, was hardly silent. He was enjoying himself immensely and loudly, drinking Red Collins's liquor and toying with the hostages, one of whom sat on his lap and played halfheartedly with Cady's thick sidewhiskers. She most likely didn't want to be there, but then, she didn't have much choice. She'd either play up to Cady, or he'd slap her around and find him someone who would. That was all part of the fun, as far as Cady was concerned.

About the only way he could be having more fun, Cady thought, was if that woman named Jewel was in his lap. And she would be, sooner or later. She was a little skinny to his mind, but she was heavy through the bust, and she had long black hair and dark eyes that made him think of long nights and feather beds.

She thought she was Miss High and Mighty because she was the mayor's daughter, and she'd never give him a glance in the ordinary course of things. But this wasn't the ordinary course of things, and when Cady decided that he was ready for her, it wouldn't matter whose daughter she was.

Cady liked getting what he wanted, and he was in a position to have just about anything he demanded. He had the power of life and death over all the town's important citizens, and before he left with a few wagons full of their gold, he was going to have his way with their women, too. He smiled in anticipation.

"You thinkin' about little Rainbow?" asked the girl in his lap.

"That's right, honey," Cady said. "I got my mind on nothin' else but you."

Mitch slipped back into Neely's livery. He could smell ashes, horse manure, and fresh-turned earth. There was a noise from the rear.

"That you, Sam?" he asked quietly.

Sam stepped out of the stall. "Yeah, Sheriff. I'm back here with your friend. I've just about finished with his burying. I'll put a horse in this stall soon as I'm done, and nobody will ever know what else is in there with him."

"Won't the horse smell him?"

"He's down too deep for that. There's pretty soft ground here till you get down to the rock. You bring me any more customers?"

"Not yet," Mitch said.

"You have a good look around?"

"Good enough."

Mitch had counted all the men he could while keeping out of sight. There were seven out in the streets, and the one in back of the saloon. If Fanny Belle's figures had been anywhere near accurate, that left around twelve inside the Bad Dog.

"What are you gonna do?" Neely asked.

"I don't know yet," Mitch answered. "I don't want Cady to start killing people."

"He's already done that," Neely reminded him.

"Any more, then," Mitch said. "Whatever I do, I have to keep Cady from knowing that I'm here."

"Maybe there could be some accidents," Neely said. "You know the kind I mean. They happen all the time in a mining town."

"Not to people who aren't mining," Mitch said.

"Folks don't have to get caught in a cave-in to get killed," Neely said. "There's lots of other ways."

Mitch saw what Neely meant. A man could fall in the rocks or get kicked in the head by a horse. But twenty men? It wasn't going to be as easy as Neely was trying to make it seem.

"We'll have to think about it," Mitch said. "Maybe between the two of us, we can come up with something."

"There's more than just us. I expect plenty of other people'd be glad to help out if they got the chance."

Mitch thought about Fanny Belle. She'd do whatever she could, as long as Rainbow wouldn't get hurt.

"You're most likely right about that," Mitch told

40

Neely. "I'll talk to a few people tomorrow, see what they think."

"I can tell you what they think."

"What's that?"

"They think it's time we took the town back from that damned Cady."

"So do I," Mitch said.

Chapter Five

Mitch was out early the next morning, making his way to the Eat Here almost as soon as the sun was up. He could smell bacon and eggs when he walked through the front of the tent, and it didn't take him more than a couple of seconds to see that there was an empty table between the place where Cady's men were sitting and everyone else.

Mitch pulled his hat down low over his face, and he sat a little apart from the others, at a table by himself. He waited for Ellie West to come by. When she did, he looked up at her and put a finger to his lips. Even at that she almost dropped the big white platter of bacon that she was carrying.

She recovered quickly, though, and said, "What'll you have?"

"Scrambled eggs and some of that bacon," Mitch said. He looked over toward Cady's men, saw that they weren't paying any attention to him, and continued. "They ever all come in at once?"

"Nope. Five or six at a time is all. You planning to do anything about them?"

"I am. I just don't know what yet."

One of the men looked up about then and yelled at Ellie: "Get your fat ass over here with that bacon."

"I hope you do it quick," Ellie said, turning away.

Mitch had almost finished his meal when Cady's men got ready to leave. They walked past his table on their way out of the tent, and one of them looked down at him.

Mitch avoided his eyes, pretending great interest in the biscuit he was using to push his eggs around on the plate.

"Hold on just a minute," the man said to his friends. "I think we got ourselves a problem here."

Mitch didn't know what the problem could be. It wasn't that he was armed, because he wasn't wearing his pistol. A lot of the miners didn't carry pistols, but just to make sure they didn't give him any trouble, Cady had ordered everyone to leave their guns at home. So Mitch had left his own Colt with Neely for the time being.

Could the man know that Mitch was the sheriff? Mitch didn't think that was very likely. So what could the problem be?

Mitch didn't have to wonder for long. The man who was looking at him said, "You're a goddamn Indian."

Mitch had hoped not to call any attention to himself. He should have known it wouldn't be possible. He looked up.

"No, I'm not," he said.

"Hell," the man said. He spit on the floor near Mitch's table. "You're worse. You're a goddamn 'breed."

43

The man was tall and fat, and he didn't look as if he'd bathed in quite a while. There were dark stains rimmed with salt under the arms of his shirt, and Mitch could smell his sour odor from where he sat.

"I don't want any trouble," Mitch said.

"Yeah," said another man, this one as skinny as a matchstick, with long hair that hung out from under his hat. "We don't need any trouble. There's no call for you to start anything, Macklin."

The fat man, Macklin, turned his head slowly, like a turtle. "I'll start whatever I want to start, Foley. You can just shut your damn mouth and let me do the talking."

Foley looked away and shifted his feet uneasily. The other three men said nothing. Their eyes were as blank as the spots on a set of dominoes.

"I don't like Indians," Macklin said to Mitch. "And I like 'breeds even less. I don't want to see you in here again while I'm eating. It spoils my breakfast."

Mitch would have liked nothing better than to shoot Macklin in his fat gut, but since he didn't have his pistol, he couldn't. Even if he'd had a pistol, he couldn't have done anything. He couldn't afford to act openly. Not while Cady was holding the hostages.

"You hear me, Indian?" Macklin said. "I'm talking to you."

"I hear you," Mitch said.

"So what are you going to do about it?"

"I'm going to finish my breakfast and not come back."

Macklin smiled, revealing tiny yellow teeth that looked far too small for his large round face.

"That's good, Indian. Because if you come back here, I'll gut you like a dressed-out deer."

He pulled a shiny Bowie knife from a scabbard on his belt and held it out for Mitch to see. The edge was sharper than Mitch would have guessed. Macklin took care of his weapons. But he was careless. Mitch was pretty sure that if he'd been in a position to act, he could have taken the knife away from Macklin and slit the fat man's throat with it before Macklin knew what had happened to him.

But Mitch couldn't make a move, even though he could feel the heat rising in him. He had to sit there and listen to whatever Macklin had to say.

But Macklin was through. He spit on the floor again, gave Mitch a contemptuous look, and walked away, with the rest of Cady's men following along behind him. Foley gave a worried glance back over his shoulder, but Mitch looked down at his plate and pretended not to notice.

When they were gone, Ellie walked back over to Mitch's table.

"Bastards," she said.

Mitch didn't think he could add anything to that, so he didn't.

"You have to do something," Ellie said.

Mitch stood up. He didn't have to pay for his meals at the Eat Here. The free meals were part of his arrangement with Reid, which Mitch figured was still in effect. He might not be acting much like it, but he was still the sheriff of Paxton.

"I'll do something," he said. "As soon as I can figure out what."

Alky didn't feel any more like a deputy than Mitch felt like a sheriff, but then, Alky was being held hostage and didn't feel much like anything. He looked around the big room that made up most of the Bad Dog Saloon. Cady and most of his men had finally gone back into the bedrooms to sleep, but Cady had left three men on guard. They didn't exactly look like they were at their best. They'd had plenty to drink the previous evening, and Alky was sure they hadn't gotten a lot of sleep.

The hostages were in even worse condition. The ones who were still asleep were sprawled on the floor, except for the banker, George Kelley, who had insisted on sleeping behind the bar.

Jewel Reid was sitting with her father at one of the tables near the piano. She looked to Alky like a woman who'd had a good night's sleep and a bath before spending an hour or two fixing herself up for the day. He couldn't figure how she managed it, since he knew her situation wasn't any different from anybody else's there in the Bad Dog. And none of them had gotten much sleep or had any time to themselves.

Alky heard a loud snore from behind the bar. Well, maybe one of them had gotten some sleep. But even at his freshest, Kelley wouldn't be much help in a ruckus. Paxton Reid might, and Red Collins damn sure would. Alky figured the saloon owner had been in many a fracas before now, and he was boiling mad about what Cady was doing to his saloon.

Alky wasn't sure about the mine owners. Sam Taylor, Harp Gooden, and Jesse Nolan had been tough enough at one time, but they were mine owners now, the biggest in town except for Reid, and they had an investment to protect. Alky had discussed it with them as much as he could, which wasn't much. Cady didn't let his hostages have much time together. But in the few words he'd managed to exchange with them, they'd made it clear that they didn't want to do anything to put their lives or their fortunes at risk.

"It's two weeks of mining," was the way Nolan had put it. "I can afford it."

The others felt pretty much the same way, and Alky guessed he didn't much blame them. If he'd had a gold mine, he might have felt the same way.

But he didn't think so, mainly because he didn't trust Cady worth a damn. Alky had known one or two men like Cady in his time, and he had a feeling that Cady wasn't going to leave the town in the same shape he'd found it. Taking the gold wouldn't be enough to satisfy him. He was going to do some other kind of meanness just because he wanted to. That was the kind of a man he was.

Alky didn't know what form the meanness would take, but he'd seen the way Cady looked at Jewel Reid. It made Alky sick to his stomach to see the way Cady's eyes changed when he stared at her.

And Alky didn't think for a minute Reid was going to sit by and let Cady have his way with Jewel when the time came. That meant that Reid was most likely going to get the hell beat out of him at the best, and get himself killed at the worst.

Even if none of that happened, Alky couldn't believe that Cady would just walk away. He'd burn the saloon to the ground, he'd kill somebody, or he'd kill somebody's dog. He was that mean. Hell, he'd already killed one of Collins's saloon girls, which was another reason Collins was practically boiling over.

The trouble was that no one except Alky seemed to

realize how dangerous Cady was. They all thought he'd just take what he wanted and leave quietly.

Alky wished Mitch were there. The sheriff would know what to do. It was too bad he'd had to go off after Carson. What Carson had done didn't seem to matter much now that Cady had come to town.

The snoring behind the bar came to a stop. Alky looked around as Kelley stood up and rubbed his eyes. There was a red mark on his face where he'd had it pressed to the floor.

Alky looked beyond Kelley to the liquor bottles that lined the wall. Alky and the other hostages hadn't been allowed to drink any, not that Alky minded much. It was awful stuff, though Cady's men didn't seem to notice.

"Good morning, deputy," Kelley said. His voice was raspy with sleep. "I don't guess Cady died during the night."

"No such luck," Alky said.

The deputy was a short, bandy-legged man with a bushy beard that covered most of his face. He scratched at his face through the beard and watched Kelley rubbing his eyes.

"Any chance we'll get breakfast this morning?" Kelley asked.

Alky shrugged. "Don't know. If Cady wants it, we'll get it. If he don't, we won't."

"Damn," Kelley said. "My belly feels like my throat's been cut."

"Maybe Cady would let you have a drink," Alky said.

Kelley looked at the bottles. "I don't think I could stand that," he said.

Alky grinned. "Don't blame you."

"You think we'll ever get out of this place?"

"Ain't sure. You wanna try to do something about it?"

Kelley was about to answer when one of Cady's men got up and pulled his pistol.

"You two shut your traps," he said.

"Yessir," Alky said.

Chapter Six

Mitch sauntered down the street in the general direction of the Bad Dog Saloon, right out in the open, not worrying about whether anyone saw him. There were two or three townspeople out and about, but not nearly as many as there would have been on a normal day. None of them looked in Mitch's direction or paid him the least attention. They were all keeping their eyes on Cady's men, four or five of whom were lounging in places that gave them a good view of the street. One of them, the one in front of the Bad Dog, was keeping a close watch on Mitch, but it didn't seem to bother him that someone was walking toward the saloon. As far as he was concerned, Mitch was just another miner, maybe one who for some reason or another hadn't gotten the word that the Bad Dog was closed to everyone except for those Cady wanted inside.

Mitch had been thinking things over for a while, but he

still didn't have a clear-cut plan. So he'd decided to walk on down the street and see if the man outside the saloon wanted to talk. Mitch didn't think there was much chance of that, but he couldn't think of anything better. And if the man didn't want to talk, maybe Mitch could get a look inside.

The man was young, with a red face and puffy eyes. He hadn't shaved in a while, but he didn't have much of a beard, just some blond fuzz on his face. When Mitch was about ten yards from him, he pulled out his pistol.

"You'd better stop right there, fella," he said.

His voice was high-pitched, and it fit his youthful face. But he wasn't smiling, and he held his pistol steady.

"Just thought I'd have me a drink," Mitch said.

"Nobody's allowed inside. Saloon's closed."

Mitch shook his head. "Never heard of it being closed before."

"Well, it's closed now. You get on back to whatever little raggedy-ass claim you've been working and forget about drinking for a while."

Mitch looked around. "I can go over to the Monkey," he said.

"That's closed, too. You go on back where you came from."

The man jerked the pistol barrel up to indicate that it was time for Mitch to move along and not waste any time about it.

"Never heard of a town without an open saloon," Mitch said.

"You have now. Get on away from here before I open a few holes in you."

"All right, all right."

Mitch turned away. He'd tried to get a look inside the Bad Dog, but the windows were too dirty, and he couldn't see anything under the batwing doors. He wondered if anyone had heard him, and if they had, whether they'd recognized his voice. Probably not.

Just as Mitch was walking away, a man came riding hard up to the saloon. He jumped off his horse and started inside. The young man leaning against the wall stepped in front of the doors and stopped him.

"What the hell's the rush, Frank? You were supposed to find Dolan."

"That's the rush," Frank said. "I can't find him. I've looked all over this damn town, and I even checked down the trail. Sherm says nobody's come down that way except me."

"Damn," the young man said. "Rance's not gonna like that."

"I know it. Now, get out of my way and let me in."

The young man stepped aside and Frank went into the saloon. Mitch started walking again. He didn't want anyone to know he'd been listening. He figured that Dolan was the man he'd killed last night. Cady was going to know now that something was wrong, but he wouldn't know what. There was no way for him to know how Mitch had disposed of Dolan. Maybe Cady would be worried, and he'd probably be mad, too. If he was, Mitch hoped he didn't take it out on his hostages.

Cady was mad all right.

"God damn it to hell," he said. "That bastard never could do what I told him. He's probably halfway back to Kansas by now."

Frank didn't think so. "Sherm says not. He says nobody came that way."

"Sherm probably slept half the night. He never could hold his liquor. I never should've sent a bottle down to him. Half the Georgia militia could've marched by there and Sherm wouldn't have known about it. If that bastard Dolan tells anybody about what's going on here, half the law in the state'll come after us."

Frank didn't see things that way. "I don't think Dolan ever left here. I think somebody did away with him."

"And who the hell would that be?" Cady asked. He waved an arm at his prisoners. "Everybody in town knows that if Dolan's dead, I'll kill some of these good people. I don't think anyone wants that. You go down there and send Sherm up here to me. If he slept all night, I'll kill him instead of these bastards."

Frank started to say something, changed his mind, and went on out of the saloon. Cady looked around at the prisoners and pulled out his pistol.

"I think I'll kill somebody just to show I'm not joking," he said. "If Dolan doesn't turn up by noon, I'll kill the damn lawman."

Alky gave a little start, but he didn't say anything.

"Hell, Rance," one of Cady's men said, "why wait? Kill the scrawny little bastard right now."

Jewel, who had been sitting at a table with her father, stood up. "You can't do that. You can't kill people just because you want to."

Cady gave her an appreciative look and then laughed. "The hell I can't. I'd like to know who's gonna stop me."

Jewel looked over at Alky, who shrugged and said, "He's the one with the pistol."

"You're goddamn right," Cady said. "And I don't mind using it. But I'll give you till noon. Dolan might just be sleeping off a drunk somewhere. What time is it, anyway?"

There was no clock in the saloon, but one of the outlaws pulled a big railroad watch from a pocket and said, "It's just about eight-thirty."

"Well, that gives Dolan plenty of time to show up." Cady turned to Alky. "You got about three and a half hours to get ready to die, pardner. That's more than a lot of men get. Maybe Dolan'll show up, but it never hurts a man to do a little praying. You'd better get started."

Alky looked at Cady as if wondering what the outlaw knew about praying, but he didn't say anything. Cady holstered his pistol.

"You keep that watch out where you can see it, Sam," he said. "Let me know when it's noon. I wouldn't want to be late with an execution."

Sam laid his watch on the bar. "I'll let you know," he said.

Cady was just as crazy and dangerous as Alky had thought he was, but knowing that he'd been right wasn't any comfort to Alky. He was pretty sure he was going to be dead in a few hours, and dead men don't get much comfort from being right. As far as Alky knew, they didn't get much comfort from anything.

Alky had heard Mitch's voice outside. That hadn't been a comfort to him, either. He knew the sheriff was back in town, and he knew that Cady wasn't aware of that little fact. But Alky didn't see how knowing was going to do him any good. Truth to tell, it was probably Mitch's fault that Alky was going to get shot, assuming that Mitch had done away with Dolan, which seemed like a pretty sure bet to Alky. It wasn't like the sheriff to find out someone had taken over the town and not do something about it.

Alky walked over to the table where Jewel and Reid sat. They hadn't said a word to each other all morning, as far as Alky knew. That was the way Cady wanted it.

Alky sat down in a chair and whispered, "The sheriff is back. I just heard him out there."

Then he got up and walked away.

Mitch went back to Sam Neely's livery. He wondered what Cady would do, now that his man Dolan had turned out to be missing. Mitch didn't know Cady, but Fanny Belle had said that Cady had killed one of Collins's girls already. It seemed likely that he might want to kill someone else now. It was up to Mitch to make sure that he didn't.

"What do you want to do, then?" Neely asked when Mitch had explained the situation. "Head for the saloon with our guns blazing like they do in the dime novels?"

Mitch didn't think that would work. Cady would kill everyone in the Black Dog before Mitch and Neely got halfway down the street. Besides, Mitch had never seen Neely with a pistol or rifle, just the shotgun he'd had the previous night. A shotgun was all right on some occasions, but this wasn't the one. Neely wouldn't have time to reload even once before one of Cady's men cut him down.

Neely wasn't serious, anyway. He knew as well as Mitch did that the two of them wouldn't get half a block before Cady killed his prisoners and then killed Mitch and Neely.

"So what's your plan?" Neely asked.

Mitch thought it over for a minute, and then he told him.

It wasn't noon or even close to it, but Alky was starting to sweat a little. Every now and then Cady would take time off from rubbing his hands on Rainbow and give Alky a crooked smile, as if to say, "It won't be long now, lawman."

Alky wondered if Cady would even wait till noon. The outlaw leader had been drinking more than was good for him, more than was good for anybody, Alky thought. Liquor didn't seem to addle Cady's mind, though. It just made him cheerful. He was still able to keep his mind on what he was doing.

The whore wasn't doing much to distract Cady, either. She seemed bored and irritated with his attentions. Alky wished he could talk to her and tell her to put a little enthusiasm into her performance. She didn't have to like Cady. All she had to do was treat him like one of her customers and show him a good time. Then maybe he'd forget what he was doing long enough for Alky to take advantage of the situation.

Around ten o'clock, Cady shoved Rainbow off his lap and stood up, steadier on his feet than he had any right to be, in Alky's opinion. He looked around the saloon and said, "To hell with it. Dolan's not coming back. I'm tired of waiting. It's time to show these goddamn miners that they can't mess around with us. Get over here, lawman."

Alky, who was sitting alone at a poker table, stood up. He didn't want to get shot, but if that's what was going to happen, he was going to be standing up for it.

"You can't do this," Jewel said. "I won't stand for it."

"Then just sit where you are," Cady told her. "There's not a damn thing you can do unless you want me to shoot you, too."

He pulled his pistol. "Come on, lawman. Don't walk so slow."

Alky said, "You sure are a mouthy bastard, you know that?"

Cady laughed. "I like a man with some gumption. Not too much, mind you, but a little never hurt anybody." He thumbed back the hammer of his pistol. "It's not going to help you, though. You been praying?"

Alky shrugged.

Cady walked over to Alky and put the barrel of the pistol up against the deputy's forehead.

"Well, if you didn't pray, you should have," Cady said.

Chapter Seven

Sam Neely didn't think of himself as a brave man, and he felt a little like a walking target as he approached the Bad Dog. The man out front watched him come toward the saloon, wearing a look of youthful contempt. He stopped Neely about ten yards away, the same as he'd done with Mitch earlier that morning.

"Hold it right there," he said, and Neely stopped.

"I got to see Cady," Neely said. "Right now."

The young man looked over his shoulder into the saloon's interior, then turned back to Neely.

"Looks like Rance is busy. He's about to plug one of your friends."

"I don't give a damn. I have to talk to him right now. He owes me money."

The young man looked interested. "You got nerve, saying that. Rance owns this town. He don't owe anybody."

58

"He owes me," Neely said. "And he better pay up. I'm not leaving here till he does."

"What's all the goddamn noise," Cady called from inside. He sounded irritated. "I got business to take care of in here."

"Fella out here says you owe him money," the young man said. "Says he ain't leaving till you pay up."

"Damn," Cady said. There was a pause. "Well, hell, it's not noon yet, anyway. I guess this can wait."

In a few seconds he stepped through the batwing doors, letting them flap behind him. He looked at Neely and then at the guard.

"Who the hell's that?" he asked.

The guard shrugged. "Damned if I know. Says you owe him money, though."

Cady looked back at Neely. "Why the hell would I owe you anything?"

"Because one of your men stole a horse from me," Neely said.

Cady opened his mouth, closed it, then opened it again and said, "I don't know what you're talking about."

"One of your men's a damn horse thief," Neely said. "That's what I'm talking about."

Cady pulled his gun. "You better start making sense fast, or I'll kill you instead of that runt inside."

"I don't know his name," Neely said. "But he was an ugly fella, 'bout your size. Had a mean way about him. Came to my livery early this morning and took the best horse I had. Said he was riding out of here, and if I wanted my money, I could ask you about it. So here I am. Asking."

"Dolan?" Cady said. "Was it Dolan?"

"I told you I don't know his name. He didn't say, and I

didn't ask. All I know is, he's one of yours, and I want to get paid for my damn horse."

"Did he say where he was going?"

"Nope. Just said he was leaving town. Headed up over the mountain, looked like."

Cady thought for a minute. "That's why Sherm didn't see him, then. Hell, I thought you couldn't get out of here that way."

"You can," Neely said, "but it's hard going."

"That son of a bitch," Cady said. "I hope he doesn't make it."

"I don't care about that, one way or the other," Neely said. "I just want the money for my horse."

"Well, you ain't gonna get it. All you're gonna get is a bullet through your gullet if you don't get away from here and leave me alone."

Neely shook his head stubbornly. "You owe me."

Cady fired a pistol shot. The bullet dug into the street by the toe of Neely's boot and sent a spray of dirt into the air.

"Next one's in your foot," Cady said. "If you can't run after that, I'll shoot you in the head."

"I guess that means you ain't gonna pay me," Neely said.

Cady nodded. "That's what I said."

Neely stood and looked at him for a second, then turned and walked back up the street. He could feel an itching between his shoulder blades in about the spot where he figured Cady's bullet would take him, but nothing happened. Neely kept walking.

"That damn Dolan," Cady said, having lost interest in Neely already. "I knew he hightailed it."

"You reckon we oughta clear out of here?" the young guard asked.

"Hell, no. This is too good to leave. Dolan might not ever make it over the mountain, and even if he does, he might keep his mouth shut. We're staying."

"That's fine with me," the guard said, but Cady didn't hear. He was already back inside the saloon.

Cady looked around the room and spotted Alky, who was standing exactly where he'd been when Cady had left.

"To hell with you," Cady said to him. "I know what happened to Dolan now, so I guess I won't kill you. Not yet, anyway. I need a drink."

He went to the bar and poured himself a glassful of the awful whiskey. After he drank it down, he said, "Where's Rainbow?"

She was sitting at a table not six feet away. "Right here," she said.

Cady briefly considered giving up Rainbow for Jewel, but he thought better of it. He wasn't quite ready. He wasn't sure just how much his prisoners would stand for. He might've gotten away with killing the deputy, but he figured that if he tried anything with the mayor's daughter, the others might try something. And if they did, he'd have to kill them.

He didn't mind that. In fact, he thought he'd enjoy it. But if he killed them, then he wouldn't have prisoners, and the town might get the idea they could attack him. He didn't want anything like that to happen.

"Come on," Rainbow," he said. He grabbed the whiskey bottle by the neck. "Let's go back to one of the rooms and take a little rest."

Rainbow didn't look happy, but she didn't resist. That was good enough for Cady.

* * *

"I don't think he killed anybody," Neely told Mitch when he got back to the livery. "Except he nearly killed me. I thought for a minute he was gonna do it for sure."

Mitch had known there was a risk. So had Neely, but he'd been willing to take the chance.

"Did you see anybody besides Cady?"

"Nope. Just that guard he has outside the door. But I guess they're all still in the saloon. From what Cady said, you don't have to worry about him doing anything to them. He thinks that fella you killed is long gone."

That was what Mitch had been hoping for. Now one man was out of the way, but as far as Cady was concerned, he was safely accounted for.

The problem was, there were still nearly twenty men left, and they couldn't be disposed of as neatly as Dolan had been.

"There's just so many men can disappear like that," Neely said, as if he'd been reading Mitch's mind.

"I know," Mitch said. "But we have to do something."

"What about smuggling some guns into the saloon? That way we'd have some help, and those folks could take care of themselves."

"I don't see how we could do that," Mitch said. "We'll have to keep picking Cady's men off, one at a time."

"Cady's not gonna like that, not one little bit."

"That's what worries me," Mitch said.

Chapter Eight

Sherm Lockett had ridden with Rance Cady for the better part of a year, and the fact that Cady had accused him of sleeping on the job really rankled him. Sure, he'd had a drink or two last night, but he'd stayed awake. That's what he'd told Cady when he called him in to ask about Dolan, and it was the God's truth. He might have shut his eyes once or twice, just to rest them, but he hadn't slept. He was sure of it.

But Cady didn't care. He'd sent him right back down the trail and told him he'd have to stay there the rest of the day, rather than coming in at noon as he was supposed to do. And Cady was going to send somebody to check on him all through the day.

"If they catch you sleeping," Cady said, "they're gonna kick your ass. And then they're gonna shoot you."

It wasn't fair, Sherm thought, wondering where the hell that damn Dolan had gone. One thing Sherm knew for sure, however: Wherever it was, Dolan hadn't come past him.

So Sherm sat there in the shade, watching the trail, hating Dolan, and wishing he had a bottle to keep him company. But he didn't have one, because Cady had taken it away from him. That Cady could be a real bastard when he wanted to.

It was a little after noon when Sherm heard the noise. The sun was just about straight overhead, and Sherm was sleepy. He might even have nodded off once, though he'd never admit it to Cady.

He was still alert, though, by God, and he knew he'd heard a noise somewhere just off the road. He stood up and looked around, but he didn't see anything unusual. There was no one coming up the road, no one coming down. There weren't even any squirrels in the trees, not that he could see.

"Damn," Sherm said, thinking that maybe he'd been sleeping harder than he thought.

Then he heard it again, a clicking sound as if two rocks had bumped into each other. This time he could tell where the noise was coming from, just across the road and off toward the little creek.

Almost as soon as he looked in that direction, he heard someone call out: "Come on over here and help me. I'll pay you."

Sherm couldn't see anybody, and he didn't like the idea of going off into the trees without knowing what he was going to find there. On the other hand, he liked being paid. It was all well and good for Cady to tell them how much money they were going to get out of the mines, but after they got it, they'd have to get it back down the

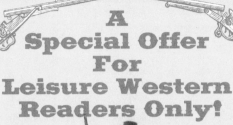

Get Four Books Totally
F R E E* –
A Value between
$16 and $20

Tear here and mail your FREE* book card today!

PLEASE RUSH
MY FOUR FREE*
BOOKS TO ME
RIGHT AWAY!

LeisureWestern Book Club
P.O. Box 6613
Edison, NJ 08818-6613

AFFIX
STAMP
HERE

mountain and off to somewhere that they could convert it into money before the law caught up with them. It wasn't going to be easy to, and Sherm thought a man with a little money in his pocket would have a better chance than a man who didn't have any.

"Come on," the voice called to Sherm. "I've twisted my ankle, and I can't get up. I'll give you five dollars to help me get up."

Anybody who had five dollars was likely to have more, and if he had a twisted ankle, he wasn't going to be able to do much to stop Sherm from taking everything he had. So Sherm decided to help himself by helping others.

He walked across the road toward the creek, looking to the right and left to be sure there was no one lurking around. He didn't see anybody lurking, but he did see a man sitting up on the creek bank, holding his hand on his ankle.

Sherm said, "Where's the five dollars?"

"I'll give it to you after I get on my feet," the man said.

Sherm wasn't going to fall for that one. "Show it to me first."

The man reached into the pocket of his jeans and pulled out a gold piece, holding it where Sherm could see it.

"Here it is. Are you gonna help me or not?"

Sherm slipped out his pistol and grinned. "I'm gonna help you, all right."

He started toward the man, his eyes on the gold. He didn't even notice when Mitch stepped out of the trees behind him, though he might have heard something before Mitch slid an arm around his neck and grabbed his right wrist, forcing him to drop the pistol. Mitch twisted Sherm's arm behind his back and up, and by then it was too late for Sherm to do anything. He didn't even have a chance to cry out before Mitch's left forearm cut off his wind.

Neely jumped up from where he'd been sitting near the creek and stood to one side as Mitch half marched and half carried Sherm down to the water. Sherm's face was turning red as he struggled to get some air into his lungs.

Just as they got to the water's edge, Mitch used his right leg to sweep Sherm's feet from under him, and Sherm fell forward toward the creek with Mitch guiding him down.

Sherm saw the water racing toward his face, and he knew what was going to happen almost as clearly as if someone had explained it to him in detail. But even knowing it, there was nothing he could do.

His face broke the surface of the water, the arm loosened on his neck, and he took a deep breath. Or he took what would have been a deep breath if he'd been standing up with his head in the air. As it was, he inhaled a great deal of water, which was never intended to fill up a man's lungs.

Sherm thrashed. He kicked. He flopped like a broken-backed snake. But he couldn't break free from the hands that gripped him and held him down. He felt as if a boulder were sitting between his shoulders, and his insides burned like fire.

Water splashed around him and bubbles popped through the surface, but Sherm's head never cleared it. After a while, not very long, his struggles became weaker. The last of his air sighed out into the creek, and he stopped moving at all.

* * *

Mitch got up from the sodden body. That makes two, he thought as he looked over at Neely, who was looking off into the trees, trying to ignore what had happened. Mitch didn't mind. Neely had done his part.

"We have to clear out all the tracks," Mitch said. "Then make one set down to the creek so it'll look like he came down here by himself. Where's the whiskey?"

"Over there," Neely said, pointing.

"We'll leave it a little way from where he's lying. It'll look like he got drunk, fell in, and drowned."

"You really think it'll fool anybody?" Neely asked.

Mitch shrugged. "I don't know for sure. But what else are they going to think?"

"I don't know," Neely said.

"Me neither. Now let's fix this up and get out of here," Mitch said. "Don't forget his pistol."

"I'll get it," Neely said.

It was around two o'clock when Frank Deevers went to check on Sherm. Seemed to Frank that he was always the one that got sent to check on people. But he didn't mind. He didn't like sitting around saloons and drinking as much as Cady seemed to.

When he got to the spot where Sherm was supposed to be watching the road, Frank didn't see anyone. That was too bad for Sherm, because Cady had told Frank exactly what to do in case Sherm had slipped off for a little nap.

"You wake him up," Cady said, "and then you kick him around a little. I don't care if he didn't let Dolan sneak off. I still think the little bastard was asleep last night."

Frank didn't like kicking people around as much as Cady did, any more than he liked hanging around in saloons, but he was going to do what Cady told him. He always did. When you rode with a man, that man was the boss, and you followed his orders. That was what Frank believed.

He got off his horse and looked around. There was no sign of Sherm, and for a minute Frank wondered if Sherm had just decided to pack it in and leave. He wouldn't have blamed him. Cady was a hard man to work for, and he'd treated Sherm like a damn fool. But that was the way Cady treated just about everybody.

But Frank kept on looking, and it wasn't too long before he found Sherm's body, lying right about where Mitch and Neely had left it. Sherm's head and shoulders were in the water, which wasn't very deep, and the rest of his body was on the bank. Frank could see the rotten tree branch that had most likely tripped Sherm up, and he could see the whiskey bottle that Sherm had most likely been nipping out of. It was easy enough to guess what must have happened.

"Got himself drunk and needed to take a pee, I guess," Frank said to himself. "Serves him right for trying to piss in the creek."

He pulled Sherm out of the water and dragged him back to the road. It was a struggle, but he managed to get the body across the back of his horse. Then he rode back up to town to tell Cady what had happened.

"God damn it!" Cady said. "That's two men I've lost today. One's run off, and the other's drowned himself."

"Looks like we're jinxed, all right," Frank said.

Cady glowered at him. "Don't ever say that."

"Sorry. I just meant that we'd had a little run of bad luck."

"It had damn well better be over with, too," Cady said. "Get your ass back down there and watch that road. If you see anybody on the way up the road, coming this way, don't ask any questions. Just kill him."

Frank nodded, though he wasn't sure he could do that. He wasn't cold-blooded as Cady.

"All right, then. Get on back down there. And Frank, if you drown, I'm gonna kill you."

Frank started to reply, but he stopped when he heard Cady laughing. You had to give Cady credit: He liked a good joke as well as the next man.

Chapter Nine

Cady sat brooding at a poker table. He was stacking chips in groups of ten and didn't seem to Alky to be paying much attention to anyone or anything. So Alky sidled over to where Jewel and her father were sitting and stood a few feet away from them. There was no one nearby except for Sam Taylor and Jesse Nolan, a couple of the mine owners. Alky wasn't worried about them.

"I bet it was Mitch that got him," he said, in a voice pitched so it couldn't be heard more than four feet away. His lips hardly moved.

Neither Jewel nor her father looked in his direction, but Reid nodded slightly to let Alky know that they'd heard and understood.

Alky moved away. No use to take chances with Cady in such a bad mood. Even his time with Rainbow hadn't helped any. And that bald-headed Gil Boone was looking at Alky funny. Alky figured Boone didn't like him much, but then that wouldn't be anything unusual. Boone didn't like anybody very much. Just at a guess, Alky had him figured to be even worse than Cady when you came right down to it, even though it was Cady who'd stuck the pistol to Alky's head and nearly pulled the trigger.

But Alky couldn't bother himself about Boone right now. As soon as Alky had heard Frank telling Cady about Sherm, he was sure that Sherm hadn't drowned by accident. Mitch must've had a hand in it. The creek was deep enough to drown in, barely, and if you were drunk it could happen. But it wouldn't be easy. Not without some help, and help was what Alky figured Sherm got from Mitch.

Alky wished there were something he could do to help Mitch along, but he couldn't think of anything. Maybe he could get a gun from one of Cady's men, though one gun wouldn't really be much help. Besides, Boone would probably kill him before he got a gun from one of the others. All he could do was bide his time and hope that Cady didn't kill anybody. And maybe hope that Mitch could do something to get them out of that damn saloon.

"Now what?" Neely asked Mitch.

They were back at the livery and Neely was pumping up his bellows. The town might be overrun by outlaws, but that didn't mean there was no work to be done.

"Now we figure out how to get rid of another one or two of them," Mitch said. "The first two were easy. I don't think it'll be that way with the others."

"I didn't like doing it," Neely told him.

"You weren't supposed to like it," Mitch said.

71

* * *

Fanny Belle looked surprised to see Mitch when he walked in her tent. She was sitting there with a drink in her hand, as usual. Mitch wasn't sure she could go more than a few minutes without one. Not that he cared. And it sure didn't seem to bother Fanny Belle.

"Should you be walking around out in the open?" she asked, motioning for him to sit down.

"I'm just another citizen," he said, sitting in the chair she had indicated. "Maybe I just want to use your services."

"This place is closed until further notice," she said, and took a drink. She set the glass on the table with a thunk. "The only customers I get are Cady's men, and they don't pay a single damn thing."

"I was wondering about that," Mitch said. "Whether they were customers, I mean. Do any of them ever come in alone?"

"Sometimes. Not often."

"Suppose two or three of them came in. Could you persuade one of them to stay a while longer than the others?"

Fanny Belle laughed, and Mitch could smell the liquor fumes all the way across the table. Light a match to her breath, he thought, and the whole tent would go up.

"I used to be able to persuade a man to do most anything," Fanny Belle told him when she'd stopped laughing and wheezing. "But that was a lot of years and a lot of pounds ago. One of the girls could do that, though. Why?"

"I'm thinking there might be an accident," Mitch said.

Three men came into Fanny Belle's tent just at dusk. They'd had supper at the Eat Here, and they'd had a few drinks in the Bad Dog Saloon. Now they were ready for an evening's entertainment.

Fanny Belle was more than willing to oblige them. "I got my best girls all eager to meet you boys," she said.

One of the men, tall, skinny, with yellowish eyes like a cat's, said, "Now, that's a damn lie for sure. Cady's got the best one of all over there at the saloon."

He looked at the others, and they all laughed. They didn't notice the way Fanny Belle's eyes narrowed at the reference to Rainbow.

"Anyway," the man said, "we ain't particular. You just give us what you got. We ain't hard to please."

"You ain't half hard any way you look at it," the man beside him said, showing jagged yellow teeth when he laughed.

"You son of a bitch."

"Now, now, boys," Fanny Belle said. "Let's not have any of that in here. No fighting in Fanny Belle's place. Just have a good time. That's what we're here for."

She called three of her girls out from the back of the tent, and the men stopped laughing when they saw them. The one with the yellow eyes rubbed the back of his hand across his mouth.

"Take your pick, boys," Fanny Belle said.

They did, and then made their way to the cots in the partitioned areas of the tent. In a few minutes, Fanny Belle could hear them grunting like rutting hogs.

It was a sound she never really got used to. But the drinking helped.

After a while they were done, and they all came out grinning like they always did.

73

"Guess I showed her what's hard and what's not," Yellow Eyes said.

"You showed her so good, I think she'd like for you to stay around a little longer," Fanny Belle told him. "If you want to."

Yellow Eyes laughed and told the others to go on without him. "I'm that much of a man. I can stay all night if she wants me to."

The others joshed with him for a minute or so and then went on. Yellow Eyes turned to go back, but Fanny Belle stopped him.

"Have a drink first," she said.

"Don't mind if I do," he said, taking the glass that she offered him. "I always did like a good drink."

You'd better enjoy this one, Fanny Belle thought. *You sure as hell won't ever be having another one.*

When Yellow Eyes got back to the cot, there was no one there. He turned angrily, but before he could yell, a girl walked in. She wasn't the same one he'd had earlier, but she was good enough.

"You wore out Star," she said. "You must be a real stud horse."

"That's me, all right," he said.

Her surprise made an O of her mouth. Then she said, "If that's so, why don't you lie down and let me give you a special treat."

Yellow Eyes had never had a woman talk that nice to him before. He lay down on the cot and started to get himself ready. But when he did, someone reached around from underneath and grabbed both of his arms.

"What the hell!" he said.

He kicked his legs and bucked, but he couldn't get free. When he looked for the girl, she was gone, but Fanny Belle was standing in the room.

"Let me up from here," Yellow Eyes said.

"Not yet, honey," Fanny Belle said, and fell down on top of him.

The cot groaned and squealed and almost collapsed on Mitch, who was underneath it, but he let go of the man's arms and slid out. He picked up a feather pillow from the floor and looked down into Yellow Eyes's face. Because Fanny Belle was lying on him with her arms wrapped around him, squeezed tight, Yellow Eyes had to struggle for breath. When he got it; he began to curse Mitch in a low, steady voice.

Mitch didn't listen. He pushed the pillow down over Yellow Eyes's face and held it there until all his struggles were over.

Chapter Ten

Gil Boone didn't like it. There was something funny about the whole thing, and it bothered him. He was fat and bald and looked a little slow and stupid, but he was neither. He knew there was something wrong, all right. He just didn't know what it was.

"There wasn't anything anybody could do," Fanny Belle was telling Cady in a pleading voice. "He just died right there in the bed with his britches off. It was like he just pleasured himself to death."

Cady looked at Boone, who shook his head. Boone thought the old whore was lying, but there was no way he could prove it. There wasn't a mark on Harve, who was lying there on the cot with his yellow eyes wide open, staring up at the top of the tent.

Boone wasn't so sure about the pleasure part, though. Harve damn sure wasn't smiling.

"Star was doing something special for him," Fanny

76

Belle said. "She told me he was enjoying himself quite a bit, and then he just hollered out something and fell back on the cot. That's all there was to it. You can see that there wasn't any fight."

Boone could see that, all right, but he still didn't like it. It wasn't natural, a man dying like that.

Cady looked down at Harve and said, "Two men dead and one run off. That strikes me as downright strange. What about you, Boone?"

"Damn right it's strange. There's something going on, Rance."

"You got any ideas about what it is?"

"Nope. You?"

"No," Cady said.

He looked at Fanny Belle, who had a glass of liquor in her hand. She looked back at him coolly and took a sip of her drink.

"You don't need to be thinking I did anything," she said. "I'm just a poor woman trying to earn a living in a rough town. I wouldn't have come and told you he was dead if I'd done anything. That being the case, I'd have taken him somewhere and fed him to the pigs."

Boone shook his head doubtfully. "I guess it could be just a case of bad things happening in threes. Dolan, Sherm, and now Harve. That might be the end of it."

Cady gave Fanny Belle a baleful stare. "It damn well better be," he said.

He clomped out of the tent, closely followed by Boone, who glanced back over his shoulder as they left. Fanny Belle, busy with her drink, gave no sign that she noticed.

When they were gone, Fanny Belle went out of the

partitioned area and put her glass on the table. Then she sat down to wait. It wasn't long before Mitch showed up.

"What am I supposed to do with that bastard in there?" she asked him. "I thought they'd at least have the decency to take care of one of their own."

"People like Cady don't think that way. Who was the other one?"

"Gil Boone. He's sort of the foreman, if you could call him that. I'd watch out for him if I were you. He figures something's wrong, but he don't know what it is."

Mitch had known that Cady or someone close to him would eventually catch on to the fact that too many people were dying or disappearing. But so far Cady had restrained himself from taking revenge. Probably because he didn't know who to take it on, Mitch thought. And sooner or later that wouldn't matter. He'd just start killing off the hostages.

Mitch wondered just how much longer he could keep eliminating people before Cady exploded into violence. Mitch had gotten rid of three men, but there were still far too many remaining for him to fight openly.

"Want a drink?" Fanny Belle asked.

"That might be a good idea," Mitch said.

About once a year Mitch tied on a really good one, got so drunk that he could barely stand up. Sometimes, in fact, he *couldn't* stand up, much less find his way home. He came dangerously close to letting it happen that evening with Fanny Belle, but something inside him clicked at just the right time and he got up from the table and walked out the back of the tent into the alley.

He couldn't think just about himself, which is what

78

he'd been accustomed to doing for most of his life. He'd had plenty of struggles, but they'd all been about his own survival. There hadn't been anyone else depending on him to get them out of a bad situation, and he'd never dreamed that there would be.

Yet somehow, by letting Reid trick him into becoming sheriff, Mitch had managed to tangle his own destiny up with the lives of so many others that he couldn't even count them.

With a whole town.

With people he didn't even know, hadn't even met.

He wasn't quite sure how it had happened, but it had. And now he had to find a way to help them. It wasn't that he cared for them, he told himself, with the exception of Jewel, and maybe Alky. But it was his job. He had to find a way to help them, and so he couldn't get drunk, and he couldn't run away.

Keeping out of sight of Cady's men, he went back to Neely's to tell him what they were going to do next.

Not more than three days after Deuce Davis had left Paxton, while the enthusiasm stirred up by his sermons was being remembered fondly, someone had suggested that what the town really needed, if it was going to be a town at all, was a church.

So George Kelley, the banker, said he'd give some money to start one. Someone else said that he knew a preacher in St. Louis who might be persuaded to come to Paxton, mainly because he didn't currently have a congregation, thanks to some misunderstanding about the proper relationship between a preacher and some of the women who sang in his choir. Not everyone was happy to think of a preacher like that coming to Paxton, but they more or less agreed that any preacher would be better than none, and that in Paxton it would be pretty damned easy to keep an eye on him to make sure he didn't stray.

So Kelley gave the money, someone wrote a letter to the preacher, and the town got started on building the church. It was only a short distance from the Bad Dog Saloon, which some people thought was appropriate and others thought was a pretty good joke on Red Collins, who was helping to pay for the church with the profits he took in from women and liquor.

On the other hand, Collins had let Davis set up in the Bad Dog when someone had burned his tent, so maybe it wasn't much of a joke after all.

What no one expected was that the new church might get burned down before it ever got finished. But it looked like that just might happen.

Luke Rutherford was the young man who'd been guarding the outside of the Bad Dog during the day, and that night he was on the street, keeping an eye out for anything out of the ordinary. Cady had told everyone to take special care because of the deaths of Harve and Sherm, so when Luke noticed the flickering light inside the partially finished church, he walked over to see what was going on.

He was still twenty or thirty yards away when he smelled the smoke.

He didn't hang around to see any more. He ran toward the Bad Dog yelling, "Fire! Fire!"

Cady and Gil Boone popped out through the batwing doors and watched him running toward them.

"Fire!" he yelled again. "Right down the street!"

"Damnation!" Cady said when he saw the flames, which by that time were spreading rapidly through the structure.

He didn't care about the town, about the people, or about any of their buildings, except for the Bad Dog. There wasn't a better place in town to put up in than the saloon, and he didn't want to lose it.

But that's exactly what would happen if the fire spread toward them, which it just might do. The wind was blowing the right way.

"We gotta do something about that fire," he told Boone.

"I don't like it," Boone said, staring down the street. "It ain't right that all this kind of stuff is happening."

"Hell, I guess you think *I* do," Cady said. "I want you to stay here and keep your gun on every son of a bitch in the place. If one of 'em so much as moves, kill him. If somebody started that fire thinking we'd let them help put it out, he's got another think coming."

Cady and Boone went back inside. "I want all my men to follow me," Cady said. "We've got a fire to put out."

He turned back to the door, and the men followed him without question. Boone watched them leaving.

It was then that Harp Gooden made a move. Of the four mine owners Cady had taken hostage, Gooden was the one least likely to settle easily into captivity. He was a man accustomed to hard work and to doing most things for himself. He'd been on his own for a long time before he finally struck it rich, and he didn't like the idea of anyone taking his ore away from him, not if there was a chance to do something about it.

There wasn't much of a chance, but there was an opening. No one was watching him, so he got out of the chair where he'd been sitting and made a jump for Boone.

He didn't get far. Boone wasn't nearly as slow as he looked. He turned as casually and as quickly as a cat, his pistol coming out of his holster in the same easy movement. Gooden had taken only two steps when Boone fired.

The shot echoed around the walls of the saloon, and smoke swirled around Boone's gun hand. The bullet struck Gooden squarely in the middle of his chest and broke on through, tearing off the right quarter of Gooden's heart.

The miner took three rapid steps backward and fell across a table, a look of awful surprise on his face. Poker chips scattered across the floor.

Cady didn't even look back.

Chapter Eleven

Mitch didn't hear the shot. He was too busy getting a little surprise ready for Cady and whoever he sent to fight the fire.

Mitch hated to have to set a fire in the church, but he didn't see any other way to get Cady outside. He wasn't even sure the fire would work, but it looked like it had. Cady was coming down the street, and most of his men were following him.

Not all of them, though. He'd left a couple behind to stand outside the Bad Dog, and Mitch figured that there were others inside.

That was all right with Mitch. He hadn't really hoped to get everyone out of the saloon, though it would have been better if it had worked out that way. Unfortunately, Cady wasn't dumb enough to leave his prisoners unguarded.

In fact, he wasn't dumb enough to walk into something

that might be a trap, as Mitch discovered when Cady stopped about halfway to the burning building and sent his men on without him.

Mitch looked toward the saloon and saw Gil Boone standing out front, waving at Cady. Boone might have been saying something, but if he was, Mitch couldn't hear it.

Cady could. He said something to his men and turned back toward the saloon. Mitch watched his back until he'd gone inside.

That was too bad, Mitch thought. He probably should have shot Cady when he had the chance, but whoever had been left behind wouldn't have liked that. And he would have had orders to take care of the prisoners if anything happened to Cady. So it was probably just as well that Cady wasn't going to be around. That way Mitch wouldn't be tempted to kill him.

But Mitch wondered what had caused Boone to call Cady back. Could he have known that Mitch was out there, just looking for his chance? Probably not. He'd just figured out that it might not be safe for Cady to be away from the saloon, and that was why he'd called him back. Well, that was lucky for Cady, but not so lucky for some of the others.

From where he was standing, Mitch watched as Cady's men, as well as a number of the townspeople who'd come running when they learned of the fire, formed up a line and started passing along buckets of water to throw on the fire.

Mitch and Neely were the only ones who knew that the fire wasn't quite as bad as it looked. They'd slipped in through the back and soaked down the inside walls of the half-built church themselves, to make sure the walls wouldn't burn too fast, and then they'd set fire to a couple of bales of Neely's hay that they'd hauled down the alley and put inside. The hay guaranteed there'd be plenty of smoke and fire. Neely would be out front to make sure no one got inside to see exactly what the situation was, and if everybody worked fast, the building wouldn't be completely lost.

But some*body* was going to get lost. Mitch was going to make sure of that.

One of the men he saw in the crowd was Macklin, the one who'd tried to start something with him at the Eat Here. If anybody deserved to have a little trouble come into his life, Mitch thought, Macklin was the one.

Mitch checked to see how things were going. Neely was up front, yelling and waving his arms to direct the people who were throwing water into the building. Fanny Belle was standing nearby, watching to make sure nobody got too close.

Mitch waited until Macklin was at the edge of the crowd, then went up to him and said, "Come on. It's starting to spread to the next building."

When Macklin turned, Mitch was already facing the other way so that Macklin couldn't get a look at his face.

"Get a couple of men and follow me," Mitch said, setting out as if he knew exactly what he was doing, which he did, though what he was doing didn't have anything at all to do with the fire.

Macklin followed, along with a couple of others. Mitch led them to the space between the church and the general store.

"Throw some water in there," Mitch said, pointing

toward one of the windows, where the fire glowed bright red.

The three men followed his directions and then went for more water. Macklin was the last to leave, and after he got a few steps away, Mitch said, "Wait a minute."

Macklin turned around, and Mitch swung the wooden bucket he was holding. He started the swing from well behind his own back, and by the time the bucket connected with Macklin's face it was traveling very fast.

Macklin might have had time to recognize Mitch, but that was doubtful. Just before the bucket hit him, he raised his eyebrows and opened his mouth, but no words came out. The bucket slammed into him like a runaway freight wagon, flattening his nose and splintering around his head.

They were still between the buildings, so no one saw what had happened. And because of the noise of the crowd and the crackling of the fire, no one heard.

Macklin lay on the ground as if he were dead, but Mitch knew that wasn't the case. He grabbed the fat man under both armpits and hauled him to his feet. Then he trundled him over to the window and stuck his head and shoulders through.

When Macklin was firmly in place, Mitch let him go and bent down to heave him inside the church. The fat man landed on the floor with a thud, and Mitch scrambled in behind him. He dragged Macklin as close to the fire as he could, then removed the knife from his boot. You never knew when a knife would come in handy. After slipping the knife into his own boot, he picked Macklin up and shoved him toward the burning hay. Macklin fell facedown into the flames.

That's four, Mitch thought as he clambered back out the window and disappeared into the night.

Jewel looked at the body of Harp Gooden. No one had moved it. It was just lying right there on the floor of the saloon where it had fallen, as if Boone didn't give a damn about what he'd done. He probably didn't, Jewel thought.

There wasn't much blood, just a little that had seeped out from the chest wound. There was a white poker chip lying by Gooden's dead hand, as if he'd been about to lay a bet and then dropped the chip when he fell.

Cady and Gill Boone were talking over by the bar. Jewel didn't know why Boone had called Cady back, but she thought maybe it had something to do with Gooden, whose sudden death had shocked everyone, though no one seemed more surprised than Sam Taylor and Jesse Nolan.

Jewel figured the mine owners thought they were immune to dying. After all, they were rich men, and they were going to make Cady rich, too, with the diggings from their mines. They thought that as long as they let him take their gold, they'd stay alive.

Now they knew that wasn't necessarily true. Of course, Gooden had made the mistake of trying to do something about his position, and neither Taylor nor Nolan seemed inclined to follow his lead. They were sitting at a table against the wall, both of them ashen, and Jewel could see that they were scared to death. Not that she blamed them.

After about an hour, Cady's men began to return to the saloon. They were tired and sweaty, but they seemed in good spirits. Jewel heard one of them tell Cady that they'd saved the building and that they all needed a drink.

While they were filling their glasses, the man leaned over and began to talk to Cady in a quieter voice. Jewel could see Cady's face getting redder and redder, so she drifted in that direction to see if she could hear what was making him so angry.

"They're saying Macklin started the fire," she heard the man say. "They say he got drunk and went in there and started it."

"Goddamn it!" Cady said. "I know that's not so. He was out there walking the streets to keep the town quiet. He didn't get drunk!"

"Well, you know Macklin. He could've had a bottle with him. It was damn sure him that they found in there after we got the fire out. Somebody drug him out in the street and left him there for everybody to see before they took him to be buried. He was burned pretty bad, but it was Macklin, all right."

Gil Boone shook his head when the story was done. "It ain't right, Rance. There's just too much funny stuff going on. That's why I called you back. It's not natural for so much to go wrong all at once."

"I know that, goddamn it," Cady said. "I want you to find out what the hell's happening, and I want you to find out right now."

Boone looked puzzled. "How'm I supposed to do that?"

"I don't give a damn how you do it. Just do it." Cady looked at Jewel, who was standing nearby. "Maybe we could kill a few more of these folks. See if that changes our luck for the better."

Boone shook his head. "I don't think that would be a good idea, Rance. If we kill all of them, who'll be the hostages?"

Cady grinned. "That's what I like about you, Boone. You look dumb as a damn rock, but you're always thinking. But wait a minute. Remind me. Wasn't it you that killed that son of a bitch lying over there?"

He turned and looked over to where Gooden's body lay on the floor.

"Hell," Boone said, "that wasn't my fault. I had to kill him. He tried to jump me."

"That's another reason you called me back, ain't it." Cady said. "You didn't want to have to be the one to kill any more of them."

"That's right," Boone agreed. "Not if I didn't have to. It wouldn't be the smart thing to do."

"All right, then. You get out there and stir things up. Check to see if it's really Macklin that's dead. And if you have to kill some son of a bitch, then kill him. We don't have to worry about anybody who's not in here. We can kill the whole damn town if we have to."

"Somebody's gotta dig that gold," Boone reminded him.

"Except for them, then," Cady said. "I'm tired of all this. What I meant was, we don't have to worry about anybody who's not working for us."

That's where you're wrong again Jewel thought. *If it's Mitch that's out there, you have plenty to worry about.*

Boone said, "All right, Rance. I'll see what I can do."

"Take your time," Cady said. "You've got all night. After that, I can't say what I might do. And get rid of that body while you're at it."

89

"Right."

Boone walked over to where Gooden's body lay and grabbed it by the left boot. He lifted the leg up from the floor and left the saloon, dragging the body along behind him. Jewel watched Gooden's head bump over the floor and disappear outside, then walked over to where her father was sitting, riffling idly through a deck of cards.

"Mitch must have killed someone else," Reid whispered when his daughter sat down. "Cady doesn't look happy about it."

"Somebody named Macklin," Jewel said. "I don't know which one he was. Do you think Mitch can get all of them?"

Reid shook his head and cut his eyes upward.

Jewel didn't look around, but she knew that someone must be coming up behind her. In a moment she could feel him there.

"You got a mighty pretty daughter, Reid," Cady said at her back. "But then, you know that, I guess."

Reid didn't say anything. He shuffled the cards he was holding and began to deal a hand of solitaire.

"I'm talking to you, Reid," Cady said, his voice hard. "You'd best answer."

Reid put a red queen on a black king and looked up. "I thought you didn't want us talking."

"When I talk, you answer. I said you got a mighty pretty daughter."

"I know," Reid said.

He didn't look up at Cady. He kept his eyes on the table and put a black jack on the red queen.

"If anything else happens to my men, I might decide

90

it's all your fault," Cady said. "I might decide to take it out on your daughter."

Reid looked up then. "That would be too bad," he said.

"Not a damn thing you could do about it, though," Cady said.

Reid put the cards he was holding facedown on the table. "No, the way things are, I suppose I couldn't."

"So if you know what's going on around here, why my men are dying and running off, you'd better put a stop to it."

"And if I don't know what's going on?"

"Then your daughter and I'll have a real nice time."

Reid looked at him for a second or two. "How can I put a stop to anything out there if I'm here in this saloon?"

"Same way you started it," Cady said. "However that was."

"And if I told you that I didn't start anything and didn't have any idea what you were talking about?"

"I wouldn't mind. It all works out the same for me. And for her."

He put a hand on Jewel's shoulder. Her skin tightened the way it might if she stepped on a snake, but she didn't move.

Reid continued to stare at Cady. "Take your hand off her," he said.

Cady smiled and removed his hand. "If you know what's going on, you can tell me right now."

Reid dropped his eyes to Jewel's. She didn't blink.

"If I knew, I'd tell you," Reid said. "But the truth is, I don't even know what you're talking about."

"I think you're lying," Cady told him. "But that's fine

with me. Maybe you'll change your mind by morning. Or maybe Boone'll find something out. If not . . ."

He left the sentence hanging, and turned to go back to the bar.

Reid watched him go with eyes as cold as a mountain winter.

Chapter Twelve

Boone dragged Gooden's body out into the street and looked up at the stars scattered across the dark night sky. The air was cool, and it seemed like a perfectly normal evening, except for the heavy smell of smoke in the air.

The smell didn't bother Boone. He walked down to have a look at the charred walls of the church, pulling the body along behind him. Gooden's head stirred up a little trail of dust in the street. There were only a few people still standing around at the church, one of whom was Luke Rutherford. When Boone arrived with his cargo, all the townspeople who were left suddenly remembered that they weren't supposed to be there and faded silently away.

"I thought you were supposed to be watching the door at the saloon," Boone said to Rutherford.

Rutherford looked sheepish. "I just thought I'd see what was going on. Nobody's tried to get into the saloon yet."

He looked down at the body. Gooden's head was now resting in a little patch of mud created by the bucket brigade.

"What happened to him?" Rutherford asked.

Boone gave Gooden's leg a little jerk, making the body twitch. "He tried to jump me. Shows not everybody in this town is gutless, as they'd like us to think. They might try to get in the saloon and get those prisoners back, for all I know. There's something going on, and Cady and me don't like it. You get your ass on back there."

Rutherford nodded toward the church. "Was it really Macklin they found in there?"

"That's what they tell me. You know anything about it?"

Rutherford grinned. "Nope. It's just that I never knew of Macklin going to church before."

"He won't be doing it again," Boone said. "I don't see him around, either. Where'd they take him?"

"Somebody said they took him to the lumber yard."

"What the hell did they take him to a lumber yard for?"

"The fella that runs it makes coffins," Rutherford said. "He's the town undertaker, I guess."

"All right. You get back to that saloon now, and keep a sharp eye out."

"I will."

"You'd damn well better," Boone said.

Evan Riley had red hair and freckles and wore a grin most of the time. He didn't look like an undertaker, and

94

he wasn't one, not really. He'd just taken on the job because he was good with his hands and could make a nice coffin. Whenever one was needed, he'd build it. It wasn't much of a step to start doing the burying as well.

Riley wasn't grinning now, however. He was looking at Mitch as if the sheriff had gone crazy.

"You can't kill all of them," he said. He looked over to where the dead men were lying in the room where he made the coffins. "This is the third one you've brought in today, but there's still a passel of them left."

"You got any better ideas?" Neely asked.

"Maybe if enough of us went up against them, we could clean them out."

"We talked about that," Mitch said. "We figure if we did, they'd kill all the hostages first."

"You're right," Riley said. "I didn't think about that."

There was a noise outside, and they all turned. Boone came stomping through the door, dragging Gooden's body along with him.

"Smells like somebody's been cooking supper in here," Boone said. He looked at Macklin's seared body. "But I guess not."

Mitch, Riley, and Neely were all looking at the body Boone had dragged in.

"You killed Harp Gooden," Neely said.

Boone gave him a glance. "That's right. He should've been more careful, but I guess he didn't think about that. Somebody said this was where the coffins got made. You the one does it?"

"No," Neely said.

"I'm the one," Riley said. He looked pale beneath his freckles.

"Well, it looks like you got a steady job around here. Seems like a lot of folks are dying." He gave Mitch a suspicious look and asked, "He one of your helpers?"

"I work at a mine," Mitch said. "I just helped Mr. Neely bring the body over here from the church."

"Which mine?" Boone asked.

"The Lucky Lady," Mitch said, naming Jesse Nolan's mine. He hoped that Nolan would be smart enough to claim him if Boone asked about an Indian who worked for him. "I guess you've heard of it."

"I've heard of it," Boone said, turning to Neely. "What about you?"

"I run the livery and blacksmith shop," Neely said. "You got any horses you need shoed, I'm the man to see."

Boone let go of Gooden's boot. Gooden's leg hit the floor, the boot heel clacking on the boards.

"Got no problem with horseshoes," Boone said. "I'm just trying to find out why so many of Mr. Cady's men are dead. You all got any ideas?"

"Not me," Riley said. "I just run a lumber yard. Make a coffin now and then."

Mitch and Neely shook their heads.

Boone didn't look satisfied. "If you change your mind, you got till morning to let me know about it. If I don't find out something by then, Mr. Cady's gonna be real mad. He might take it out on your town. He might even take it out on those friends of yours up at the saloon. That young woman is looking mighty good to him."

Mitch felt his stomach muscles tighten.

Boone spit on the floor beside Gooden's head. "I don't give a damn what kind of a coffin you make for this one. But you be sure the ones you make for our boys are the best you can do. You hear me?"

"I hear you," Riley said.

"Good."

Boone turned to leave, but before he got outside, he turned back.

"You know," he said to Mitch, "they tell me an Indian's bad luck. You think you're bad luck?"

I will be to you, Mitch thought, but he didn't say it. He said, "No, I don't think so. I'd say I was good luck for all concerned."

"Yeah," Boone said. "I can see where you'd think that. Sure don't look that way to me, though. I guess we'll find out, won't we?"

"I guess we will," Mitch said.

"Now what?" Neely said as soon as Boone was gone.

Mitch put his finger to his lips. He walked over to the door and looked out. When he'd made sure that Boone wasn't hanging around outside, he said, "After what he said, we might have to change our plans."

"I knew we couldn't keep taking Cady's men one at a time," Neely said. "They were bound to catch on."

"They haven't caught on yet," Mitch told him. "I don't think they know what's happening. They're just suspicious."

"They killed Gooden," Neely pointed out. "That means they're more than suspicious. They're dangerous."

"We knew that already," Riley said. "Gooden wasn't the first one they killed."

"Yeah," Neely said. "But what are we gonna do about it?"

"We might have to change our plans," Mitch said.

"How?"

"We might have to try to get them all at once."

"You just said that wouldn't work," Neely pointed out.

"I've changed my mind," Mitch said.

Chapter Thirteen

Alky had heard what Cady said to Jewel, and he didn't like it a bit. He didn't like the way Cady had put his hand on her, either. He knew he wouldn't be able to sit by and let Cady have his way with her, any more than Reid would.

Reid had a better claim to his feelings for Jewel than Alky did, but the deputy couldn't help the way he felt. Jewel had treated him right from the first time he met her. It wasn't every pretty woman who'd treat a little bandy-legged coot like he was just as good as she was.

There was something else that Alky had to consider, however. He knew that Mitch was out there somewhere in town, and he knew that the sheriff was most likely responsible for the men who'd died. He wondered if there was some way to get word to Mitch about what Cady was thinking, but he couldn't think of one.

Mitch needed some help, but Alky couldn't give it to

him. The only advantage he had was that he knew Mitch was out there and Cady didn't. Leave it to Mitch, being half Indian, to come up with the idea of killing off Cady's boys one at the time. It was a good idea, but it was too bad Cady seemed to be catching on.

One thing for sure, it had Cady worried. He was drinking more than ever, and he wasn't even interested in Rainbow anymore.

That could be a bad sign, though, Alky thought. It might mean that Cady was saving his energy for Jewel. Alky didn't like that idea one little bit, but there wasn't anything he could do about that, either.

There was one other thing that worried him. Jesse Nolan and Sam Taylor had walked over to the bar and started talking to Cady, who hadn't wanted to listen to them at first. But after a while, he got downright friendly with them and even offered them a drink. Alky didn't know what to make of it, but he knew he didn't like it.

They were still jawing after midnight, and George Kelley was getting crotchety because he couldn't get behind the bar to go to sleep. He said he couldn't sleep out in the open like the others had to do, or in a chair like Jewel could.

"I'm the kind of a man that needs his privacy," he told Alky. "I don't see why they can't shut down and go to sleep like normal people."

"Because they ain't normal," Alky said. It amazed him that Kelley could even talk about what was normal in a case like this. "If you talk to Cady, maybe he'll let you have one of those feather beds that Red's girls use."

"You think so?" Kelley said.

"Hell, no," Alky said. "I was joshing you. You oughta

just go lie down in a corner if you need to sleep so bad. Now hush up. Cady's looking this way."

Kelley hushed, but he didn't go find a corner. He walked over to a table, sat down, and started stacking poker chips. Red Collins was sitting across from him, watching.

One thing Alky had to say for Collins: He was keeping calm. So were Reid and Jewel, though Alky wasn't sure whether they were really as calm as they looked or if they were just putting on a good appearance.

Rainbow was in one of the back rooms, asleep. Cady seemed to trust her for some reason. Maybe he didn't think he was in any danger from a whore.

And maybe that was where he was wrong. Alky wondered if Rainbow could sneak out and get word to Mitch that they knew what he was up to. It seemed like a good idea until Alky realized that Cady would have somebody back in the alley, watching in case anyone tried to get out that way. And if someone did get out and get away, Cady would probably start acting crazy and shoot somebody. Or have Boone do it.

While Alky was thinking along those lines, Boone came into the saloon, the batwing doors flapping behind him.

Cady looked up, saw him, and sent Taylor and Nolan packing. He didn't seem to have any more use for them. As soon as they were away from the bar, Cady and Boone got into a deep conversation. Alky thought about seeing if he could sneak over close enough to hear, but one of Cady's men gave him a look, so he kept his distance.

Alky found a chair and dragged it over to the wall. He sat in it and tilted it back until it rested against the wall. He was about as comfortable as he was going to get. He looked at George Kelley, who was practically wringing his hands. Too bad, Alky thought, and closed his eyes.

"There's plenty of dynamite in a mining town," Neely told Mitch. "We could just blow up the damn saloon."

"Red Collins wouldn't be too happy about that," Riley said.

Riley didn't know exactly how he'd become part of the small conspiracy that involved Mitch and Neely, but he'd been drawn into it. He didn't mind, though. He didn't like the idea of the outlaw takeover any more than they did.

"Yeah," Mitch said. "If we blew up the saloon, it might be a big surprise to Red, especially since he's in it. Along with a lot of other people who don't need blowing up. Reid's there, too. I don't much like him, but I'd hate to see him go. He's the one who pays my salary."

"Those damn hostages," Neely said. "That's the whole trouble. If Cady didn't have them, we could take him down easy."

Riley said, "If that's the trouble, then we have to get the hostages away from him."

Neely was skeptical. "We know that. But what we don't know is how we can do it. We can't figure out how."

"Maybe you're looking at it the wrong way," Riley said. "The fire was a good idea, but it didn't quite work out like you planned it, did it?"

"No," Mitch said. "I thought Cady might commit all his men to fighting it, maybe even come himself. He started to, but then he didn't."

"Too damn smart for us," Neely said.

"It was Gil Boone," Mitch said. "Boone was in the saloon, and he called Cady back."

"Doesn't matter who it was," Riley pointed out. "The fact is, you didn't get Cady, and the prisoners didn't get loose."

Neely looked over at where Gooden's body lay. "One of them tried. Didn't do him any good."

"The way I see it," Riley said, "we've just got one thing in our favor, and that is that they don't know what's going on. They don't even know Mitch is here. Or who he is. They think we're just a town of cowards."

Neely bristled. "We're not cowards. We just don't want anybody to get hurt. Besides, Gooden and Nolan and Taylor told all their men not to try anything, just work the mines and turn the gold over to Cady."

"Why don't we just do that, then?" Riley asked. "After he gets what he wants, Cady will just go away and leave us in peace."

"You don't really believe that, do you?" Neely said.

Riley shrugged. "I'm not sure. He might."

Neely looked at the sheriff. "What do you think, Mitch?"

"Cady'll kill the hostages and burn the town," Mitch said. "That's what I think."

"I think you're right," Neely said. "We got to do something."

"Well, I can help you out," Riley told them. "Maybe."

"How?" Mitch asked.

"I helped build that saloon. I know some things about it that nobody else does."

"How is that going to help us?"

"Maybe it won't," Riley said. "But I'll tell you if you want to hear it."

"We're listening," Mitch said.

* * *

Cady was a little drunk. Boone didn't ever remember having seen him like that, and he didn't like it much. It made him uneasy. Cady was always calm, always in control. But something was bothering him, and Cady wouldn't tell Boone what it was.

What he did tell him was that he wanted a better guard on the saloon: "Two men in the alley out back. Two out front. Two in the back rooms. Two at those windows up front. That leaves you, me, and five men to patrol the streets. Make sure they stick close. No need for them to go off looking for trouble. If trouble wants us, it'll find us right here."

Boone got everything organized. It didn't take long, and he didn't even wake up any of the sleepers. Then he went back to where Cady was sitting at the bar.

"I wish to hell you'd tell me what's bothering you," he said.

Cady drank whiskey from a thick glass and said, "It might not be anything. I just think that with all that's been happening, we need to be a little more careful."

"You think anybody's tried to sneak by Frank down there on the road?"

"No. I just think we've been spreading ourselves too thin. It's time to pull in our horns and let things work for us."

"What things?"

"We've got the miners in our pocket, except for the one you killed. And that damn Reid. In another week, we'll have more gold than we ever dreamed of. All we have to do is sit tight and let it come to us."

"Sounds good," Boone said, but for the first time he

was thinking that Cady's whole scheme sounded too good to be true. Maybe Cady's idea hadn't been quite as good as it had sounded when he'd first heard it. When your men start dying and running off, it's not a good sign.

"Get some sleep," Cady told him. "You might need it."

Boone nodded. Sleep sounded good to him. It would be a good way to quit worrying about things.

"That Rainbow's back there in a room," Cady said. "If you're not too sleepy."

Boone grinned. He wasn't as sleepy as he'd thought he was. Not as worried, either. A woman could take care of a lot of things.

Chapter Fourteen

It wasn't easy to decide whom you could trust, Mitch thought. The truth was, he didn't know many people in Paxton well, and a whole lot of them he didn't know at all. When you came right down to it, the ones he knew best were out of reach, held captive by Rance Cady in the Bad Dog Saloon. All the others in town might be fine people, and they might be entirely trustworthy, but Mitch didn't know them well enough to be sure.

Mitch trusted Neely because of what the blacksmith had done already. Neely had been willing to help when he was needed, and he didn't ask questions.

Riley had fallen right in with them when he was needed, too, so Mitch figured Riley could also be trusted. That made three of them.

Three people against fourteen, though, wasn't exactly good odds.

So Mitch had suggested asking Fanny Belle to help

out. Neely and Riley had been against the idea, but Mitch convinced them to talk to Fanny Belle before they made up their minds, so they sneaked into the back of her tent and asked her what she thought.

"I can shoot a gun just as well as any of you sons of bitches," she said, pouring herself a drink. "Any of you want a little snort?"

It was well after midnight, and all her girls were gone, but Fanny Belle lived on the premises.

"We don't need to be drinking," Mitch said.

Fanny Belle took a swallow. "I do."

She always did, Mitch thought. But if she wanted a drink, it was all right with him. It never seemed to affect her.

"If you don't mind my saying so, you don't look like much of a fighter," Neely said.

"Well, I do mind your saying so. Looks don't tell everything about a person, you know. And that goddamn Cady's got something I want."

"What?" Riley asked.

"None of your business. Don't matter, anyhow. If you want somebody who can shoot and fight, you've come to the right place. Just tell me what you want me to do, and I'll do it. You hear?"

"We hear," Mitch said. He looked at the other two. "What about it?"

Riley shrugged. "We don't have a lot of choice, do we?"

"Not that I know of," Mitch said. "I think Fanny Belle will be fine."

"Damn right, I will," she said. "Who else you got in on this?"

"Nobody, so far."

"Well, you need a few more. I got a name for you."

"Who?" Mitch asked.

Fanny Belle drained her glass. "Ellie West."

"Hell," Neely said. "Another woman?"

"What's the matter with you?" Fanny Belle asked. "You think a woman ain't tough enough for the job? Let me tell you something, every girl I got has more guts than all the men in this town put together. If they didn't, they wouldn't be able to earn a living the way they do. When it comes to being tough, men don't know a goddamn thing. They just think they do. And that damn Cady has somebody that Ellie cares about. A woman will fight for what she cares about, in case you never noticed."

"Sorry," Neely said. "I wasn't thinking."

"You oughta try it sometime," Fanny Belle told him. "It wouldn't hurt you."

Mitch grinned at the exchange. He hadn't thought about Ellie West, but now that Fanny Belle had mentioned her, it seemed like a good idea.

"Let's go talk to Ellie," he said.

Ellie West lived in the back of the tent that served as her café. She didn't take too kindly to being awakened in the middle of the night by a tall man standing over her bed, but when Mitch struck a match and let her see his face, she got into a better mood.

"You nearly scared the life out of me," she told him. She sat up and pulled the covers up to cover herself. "I thought you were probably one of Cady's men. What on earth are you doing here?"

"Looking for help," Mitch said. "Fanny Belle said I should talk to you."

"What kind of help?"

108

He told her. "Do you think you could do anything along those lines?"

Ellie was a large woman, but not in the way that Fanny Belle was large. She was tall and broad-shouldered, and the hands that held her covers wouldn't have looked out of place on someone working the mines.

"I'll tell you a little story," she said. "When I was about twelve years old, a boy named Jimmy Green grabbed me out behind the little one-room school I was going to. He didn't go there. He was older, and he never spent a day inside a school, as far as I know. I don't have to tell you what he had in mind. He never got it, though. What he got was a finger in his eye, a bloody nose, and a knee where it did the most good. I do believe he walked in a crouch for the best part of a week after that. Anything else you want to know?"

"Can you use a gun?"

"Can a cow chew her cud? Of course I can use a gun."

"You'll do," Mitch said.

"Damn right, I will. Now, get out of here and let me get dressed."

The plan was simple. They were going to surprise Cady, get the drop on him before he and his men could kill anybody. They were going to do it by getting inside the Bad Dog before anybody knew they were there.

It was Riley's idea. When the saloon was built, Red Collins had asked Riley for a few special things. One of them was a secret entrance.

"He wanted it in case he ever needed to get out quick," Riley explained. "It's in back of the bar. I don't think anybody knows about it except for me and him."

"If it's there, why ain't he used it?" Fanny Belle asked.

The five of them were gathered in the coffin room of Riley's lumber yard. The four corpses lay on one side as a reminder of what could easily happen to them all.

"I don't think he can get to it, what with all Cady's men around. It was something he'd use if he could see trouble coming. It didn't work out that way with Cady. He got there before Red knew what was happening."

"The question is, can we use that way to get in?" Mitch said.

"I don't see why not," Riley told him. "It's just like a door—it opens both ways."

"But it's under the building," Neely said. "Which means we have to get under there to use it."

Riley nodded agreement. "Right. But if someone's going in through the back, we'll have to deal with whoever's on guard in the alley. That'll be the first thing. When that's done, we can go under the building."

Mitch's idea was to strike from three positions. Two people would go in from the back, assuming the guards could be dealt with. One person would go through the door in the floor that Riley had told them about. And two would come in from the roof, where Riley had said there was another door.

"The roof should be the easy part," he said. "We can get to it from the next building."

"If those men in the alley don't hear us," Ellie said.

"It all comes back to them," Mitch agreed. "We have to get them out of the way first. After that, it's a matter of timing and surprise."

It was the surprise they were counting on. They were going in during the deepest darkness of the night, when everyone in the saloon would be sleeping, or at least sleepy. There hadn't been any trouble for Cady so far, so he shouldn't be expecting any. His men would be lazy and relaxed.

Or so Mitch hoped. He wasn't encouraged by what he'd seen so far that night. Cady had pulled his street patrol back to the saloon area, and he'd set out another guard in front. Mitch wasn't sure what all that was about.

"Cady couldn't know anything, could he?" Neely asked, as if he knew what Mitch was thinking. "He couldn't know we're coming."

"I don't see how," Mitch said. "We didn't know it ourselves until a couple of hours ago, and nobody's been down to the saloon to talk over our plans with Cady."

"You're right," Neely said. "I guess I'm just edgy."

"I don't blame you," Riley said. "I am, too. This isn't the kind of thing I deal with every day. I do more in the way of making coffins than in trying to kill people to fill them."

Neither of them said so, but Mitch could tell that another thing bothering them was the presence of Fanny Belle and Ellie. They didn't like the idea of having to depend on women when shooting was going to be involved.

"I'd hate to wind up like those fellas over there," Riley said, looking at the bodies. "And if I get killed, who's gonna bury them? For that matter, who's gonna bury me?"

"Somebody'll take care of it, don't you worry," Fanny Belle assured him. "We'll see to it that you get taken care of, too."

"You'll need a new coffin maker if you do."

"We'll find one. I'd say that's the least of your worries."

"You're probably right about that," Riley agreed.

"Cady's going to kill those people if we don't do something," Ellie said. "We can't be worrying about ourselves. The worst thing that can happen is that we'll get killed, and he'll go ahead and do what he was planning to do all along. But if this plan works out, we can save them. So we have to make it work."

"We'll try," Mitch said. "Let's check out our firearms."

Mitch was planning to be the one who came in from underneath the saloon, which he thought would be the most dangerous job. He had his own Colt and another he'd taken from his office. He would have taken a rifle, but he thought it might be too cumbersome to try bringing it in the way he was going.

Fanny Belle had a shotgun. She knew how to use it, as Mitch had reason to know from previous experience. She and Ellie would go through the back of the saloon. They didn't want to do the climbing necessary to go in from the roof.

"You better take care not to let that thing go off and hit the wrong people," Neely told Fanny Belle. "A scattergun can be trouble in a tight place."

"I'll take care of my business," Fanny Belle said. "You take care of yours."

She inserted two cartridges in the weapon and snapped it shut.

Neely had a brace of Smith & Wesson Schofield .45s. Mitch was surprised that the blacksmith had pistols like that.

"If they was good enough for Jesse James," Neely said, "they're good enough for me. Not that I ever used them the way Jesse did."

Mitch didn't inquire any further. When a man came to a place like Paxton, no one looked too closely into his past.

Ellie West wasn't much for pistols. So she had a Winchester and a little Remington over-and-under .41 derringer that she carried with her every day.

"Just in case there's any bad trouble at the Eat Here," she said. "I can use it for close work."

"Pays to be ready for that kind of thing," Riley said. He had a Colt's Frontier model and a Winchester, which he held out in front of him and looked at. "I generally use this for hunting, but I haven't hunted in a long time."

"What do you think we're gonna be doing?" Fanny Belle asked.

Riley thought it over. "I guess you're right," he said.

Chapter Fifteen

Mitch crouched beside the barrel in the alley behind the Bad Dog Saloon, hardly breathing. He was sure no one could hear him, certainly not the guard that Cady had back there. When he'd been a scout, Mitch had learned the value of silence. He figured it was around three o'clock, though he didn't know for sure. He didn't carry a watch.

He knew where the sentry had been on his earlier visit to the alley, but he wasn't sure that the man hadn't changed places since then. His plan was to wait until the man got careless and had another smoke. Then he'd deal with him. He hoped he wouldn't have to wait for long.

As it turned out, he didn't. The man's lack of discipline gave him away again, though Mitch couldn't really blame him. He or someone else just like him had been standing in that same alley for several nights now, and no one had tried to get into the saloon from back there. There was no reason for him to think things were going to change any-time soon.

If he'd been a professional, like some of the men Mitch had known when he was scouting for the Army, it might have been different. Mitch knew men who could stand night guard for weeks on end, if need be, without ever lighting a smoke, though when they were off duty they smoked all the time.

But this man wasn't a professional, he was just an owl-hoot, and not a very bright one at that. Mitch watched the glowing tip of the cigarette until it disappeared as the man turned aside. And when he turned, Mitch moved.

He came up behind the man silently as settling dust and put a forearm around his neck. Whatever sound the man might have made was choked off as Mitch tightened his arm and locked it into place. The man's feet kicked back feebly against Mitch's legs, but Mitch pulled his arm even tighter, and the kicking didn't last long.

When the man went limp, Mitch lowered him to the ground. But before he could turn, he heard someone at his back: "Don't turn around, you sorry son of a bitch. If you do, I'll blast you."

Mitch cursed himself for an idiot. He'd spotted the extra guard out front earlier, and he should have known there might be an extra one at the back as well. Again he wondered why Cady would have taken such precautions.

"What'd you do to Bob?" the man behind Mitch asked.

"Nothing much," Mitch lied. "He's a little out of breath, but he'll be all right."

"He damn well better be. Now, let's get you inside so

115

we can see just who the hell you are. Rance'll be interested to hear why you were sneaking around back here. Hold still while I take care of your gun."

The man came closer, but he was careful not to get too close. He reached out and slipped Mitch's Colt from the holster. He put it on the ground, then patted around until he found the second pistol stuck in Mitch's belt. He slid that one out, too.

"All right," the man said. "Let's go. Just walk straight down the alley."

Mitch wanted to go inside the saloon, but he didn't want to go in at gunpoint, with his own weapons lying in the alley. He took a couple of steps, and his left leg appeared to give way under him.

"What the hell?" the man behind him said.

Mitch straightened back up. He was now holding Macklin's knife, which he'd removed from his boot. If the man had been a professional, as he'd already proved he wasn't, he'd have checked Mitch's boot, too. Mitch always checked boots these days, though it was a lesson he'd learned only recently.

"Turned my ankle," he said. "It's dark back here."

"Not so dark that I can't see where you are. You just keep moving."

"Sure," Mitch said.

He took another two steps before he suddenly whirled and threw the knife at a point just below where he believed the man's face to be.

There was a fleshy *thunk* as the knife struck. The man had time for only a blood-bubbling gasp before Mitch was on him, bearing him quickly to the ground and wrenching his pistol from his hand.

The knife was in the man's throat. Mitch jerked it out, turned the blade, and slashed the throat from side to side. Arterial blood pumped out of the gash. Mitch jumped aside to avoid as much of it as he could.

Two men were dead now. Mitch hoped there hadn't been enough noise to disturb anyone inside the saloon. He went to find his pistols, doing some subtraction in his head. The way he figured it, Cady couldn't have more than fourteen men left. If one of them was down guarding the road, that meant only thirteen were still in town.

Five against thirteen, he thought. The odds were getting better all the time. Not exactly what you'd want in a high-stakes poker game, but they were improving.

Mitch figured that was about all he could ask for.

Rainbow thought she heard something in the alley, some kind of scuffle, but she didn't let on. If someone was out there messing with the guards, she wasn't going to be the one to let anybody know. For all she cared, Cady and his men could go straight to hell. It couldn't happen soon enough to suit her. All she cared about was getting out of the Bad Dog and back to Fanny Belle. Fanny Belle understood her.

Gil Boone was on top of Rainbow, panting and snorting and red in the face, and she was sure he didn't hear a thing, not even his own animal noises. Men never did when they were acting that way. It would be over soon, and maybe she could get some rest.

Or maybe she wouldn't get any rest at all. Maybe someone was out there in the alley, someone who'd come in and rescue her. She'd about given up on that, however, and she had a pretty good idea what was going to happen

117

to everyone when Cady got what he wanted from the mines.

She just hoped she'd have a chance to do a little damage to them before they killed her. They didn't know it, but she had a little surprise for them. She always carried a long hatpin in her hair, and no one had noticed it when they'd searched her. They'd made dirty jokes about how thorough their search was, and about how they'd looked in all the nooks and crannies, but they hadn't even thought of her hair. Stupid bastards. When the time came, she wasn't going to go easy. She was going to put up a fight.

She'd had at least one chance to kill Cady. Hell, she could maybe kill Boone right now. But what good would it do? Someone would just kill her. She was saving the hatpin for a time when it might do a little more good.

She strained her ears, trying to hear any other sounds that might come from the alley, but all she could hear was Boone.

She closed her eyes and tried to pretend she was somewhere else, somewhere that Gil Boone and Rance Cady didn't exist.

It didn't work, so she tried to imagine what Boone would do when he was finished. She wondered if he'd pay.

At that thought, she almost smiled.

It took ten minutes after killing the guards for Mitch to get everyone in position. Now that the alley was clear, it wasn't hard to do.

Neely and Riley went up to the roof of the general store by climbing a ladder that they brought from the lumber yard. Fanny Belle and Ellie went to the back of the Bad Dog with Mitch. They stood and watched as Neely and Riley laid the ladder across the alley between the store and the saloon and crawled across.

When the two men were safely on top of the saloon, Mitch waved his arm. From that moment, everyone was supposed to begin counting. After they'd all counted to a hundred three times, if all was going right, Mitch would come out behind the bar of the saloon. Fanny Belle and Ellie would come in through the back. And Neely and Riley would come down from above.

Mitch knew that the chances of all of them hitting three hundred at the same time were fairly small. He hoped it wouldn't matter. As long as they all arrived at nearly the same time, everything would work out.

At least that's what he told himself as he slipped under the saloon floor and scooted off in the general direction of where the secret trapdoor was supposed to be.

Probably should have looked for it when I was here before, he thought.

It was too late to worry about that now.

What if the trapdoor's locked on the inside? he wondered.

Too late to worry about that, too.

Counting and scooting, smelling dirt and dampness, he moved forward.

Chapter Sixteen

Fanny Belle was counting for herself and Ellie, who stood close by, watching Fanny Belle's lips moving. Ellie wasn't sure where Fanny Belle was in the count, but the other woman had promised to let her know before doing anything.

After a while, Fanny Belle's lips stopped. She looked at Ellie and nodded. Ellie got her Winchester ready.

They knew how they were going in. There was a door not far from where they were standing. It was sure to be locked, but that didn't matter. They had a plan that took locked doors into account.

Fanny Belle looked at Ellie, who nodded and pointed the shotgun at the door.

"Ready?" she asked.

Ellie nodded again, and Fanny Belle pulled the trigger.

* * *

Mitch heard the blast just as he found the trapdoor. He'd wound up going past it and having to turn back, but by his count he still had another few seconds. Fanny Belle's count must have been a little faster.

Mitch grabbed the handle and heaved up on the trapdoor.

It moved about a quarter of an inch upward, then dropped back in place. There was something on top of it, something heavy.

"Goddamn it," Mitch said to no one in particular.

He turned over on his back, put his boots against the door, and shoved. The muscles corded in his legs. The door moved steadily upward, slowly at first and then much faster as something rolled off it. Mitch stood up and came through it in a rush.

He saw George Kelley cowering off to one side, shaking his head as if he was wondering what the hell was going on. Kelley must have been on top of the trapdoor, Mitch thought, not bothering to wonder why.

"Here," Mitch said, tossing him a pistol. "Use it."

Kelley fumbled the pistol as if it were hot. Mitch didn't wait to see what the banker did after that. Looking over the top of the bar, he scanned the room.

He couldn't see Jewel or Cady, but the room was already full of gunsmoke. Handguns were going off all over, and rifles were firing from above and to the side.

Mitch spotted Reid over near a wall. Reid had acted fast, pulling over a poker table and taking cover behind it. He wasn't going to die stupidly if he could help it. Alky dived back there with him, and Red Collins had found a table of his own.

One of Cady's men was crouched down in back of the

upright piano, shooting at all three of them. Bullets chipped big splinters off the tables and sent them flying.

Mitch took a shot at the man, but his bullet went wide and spanged into the piano. Mitch could hear the discordant sound of piano wires breaking even over the gunfire.

The man turned and fired a round at Mitch, and a bullet nearly parted his hair. It crashed into a bottle in back of the bar, and another bottle burst almost at once. Mitch fired back at the man, but Ellie West had already picked him off with her Winchester. He fell in back of the piano, and all Mitch could see of him was a cheap pair of boots.

Mitch nodded at Ellie, who grinned back.

Riley and Neely were in the upper hallway, shooting down and wreaking havoc. They had the angle and the advantage, and Cady's men were falling all around. Mitch had to give them credit: They might be on the wrong side of the law, but they weren't cowards.

The men who'd been outside came rushing in, and all of them faced devastating fire from several different directions at once.

Mitch shot one man as he came through the batwings. The man fell backward and out. The man who had preceded him turned toward Mitch, who shot him in the face. He hit the floor and didn't move.

Even Kelley joined in the fighting and got off a couple of rounds. Mitch didn't think he hit anyone, however.

Three men rushed Fanny and Ellie. Fanny got two of them with one blast of the shotgun, tearing big hunks of their sides away and felling them on the spot. Ellie got the third with the derringer just as he closed on them.

Through the swirling smoke, Mitch had time to notice

that Rainbow was standing just behind Fanny Belle, a fierce grin splitting her face, just before Luke Rutherford tried to lunge over the bar. Mitch shot him in the chest, and the young man fell backward.

Mitch jumped over the bar and kicked the pistol out of Rutherford's hand. Luke stared up at him with lifeless eyes.

Across the room one of Cady's men started to raise his head. Alky slammed it back to the floor with a chair.

And then it was all over. No one moved in the room. Mitch hardly noticed the silence. Gunshots were still ringing in his head.

"You've made a hell of a mess in my saloon," Red Collins said. His voice seemed to echo hollowly. "Thanks."

"It's about damn time you got here," Alky said. "But you're about a half hour too late."

"Where's Jewel?" Mitch asked. "And Cady."

"That's what he means about you being late," Reid said, standing up. "They're gone. Cady took Jewel and left. Nolan and Taylor went with him."

Neely and Riley came down from above, while Ellie West walked over and stood by Reid. Rainbow sat down, and Fanny Belle fussed around her like an old hen.

Mitch looked at the bodies on the floor. He counted eleven. Not all of them were dead, but those that weren't wouldn't be sitting a saddle anytime soon.

"Boone?" he asked.

"He went out the window in the back," Rainbow said. "I don't know how far he'll get. He's not wearing any pants, and he don't have his boots on."

"Good," Mitch said, thinking that Boone hadn't shown much loyalty to his boss. But then, from what Alky said, Cady hadn't shown much loyalty to Boone, either.

"Maybe we can catch up to him. Riley, you and Neely go have a look-see."

Without a word, the two men left by the back way.

Mitch turned to Reid. "Why the hell did Cady leave?"

"It was my fault," Alky said. "At least I guess it was."

"How?"

"I said something to Reid about you being the one causing the trouble in town. Nolan and Taylor must've heard me, and I think they told Cady."

"Damn," Mitch said.

"They were afraid he was going to kill them when all this was over, I guess," Alky said. "Hell, he probably was. Boone shot Gooden earlier, and that really scared them. So they figured to buy their lives by telling Cady about you."

"That's when he decided that he didn't want to have everybody in the same place," Reid said. "He took Jewel and left. He made Taylor and Nolan go, too."

"Probably killed them by now," Alky said. "No better than they deserve, if he has. Goddamn traitors is what they are."

"They were just yellow," Mitch said.

He'd seen men turn coward before, and it no longer surprised him. Sometimes the very man you thought would stand by you through hell and high water was the first one to cut and run when things got rough.

"The thing is," Reid said, "what are you going to do about it?"

"I'm going to find them," Mitch said.

"How're you gonna do that?" Alky asked.

"I don't know," Mitch said, "but I will."

"You'd better," Reid said.

Chapter Seventeen

Cady heard the shooting back at the saloon and knew he'd done the right thing by leaving. Sure, he could have stayed and killed all the hostages, but where would that have left him? Without a bargaining chip, that's where. This way, no matter how things turned out, he could still bargain.

Things were going bad, but Cady knew it wasn't his fault. It was just like some damn half-breed sheriff to come sneaking into town and kill his men like that. Cady couldn't understand what kind of a mayor would hire a 'breed in the first place, but Taylor and Nolan had assured him it was true. Cady knew what Indians were like, and picking his men off one at a time like that was a typical Indian trick.

But Cady wasn't going to let the sheriff ruin his schemes. If his men could handle things at the saloon, well, that was fine; if they couldn't, that was their lookout. As for Cady, he was still planning to clean out the town before he left, with them or without them. It didn't really matter much.

It could still be done, Cady figured. Maybe not as easily as he'd thought, but he could still pull it off. He had two of the miners on his side now. All they wanted was to get out of the mess they were in any way they could, as long as their worthless hides were in one piece. They'd promised him they'd even help him out, let him stay at one of their camps until the gold was loaded up.

It sounded all right to Cady. He had the woman as his security. If anyone tried to stop him, he'd kill the woman. That damn half-breed would think twice before he risked that. She wasn't just the mayor's daughter. She was about the only good thing in the whole damn town, if you didn't count the gold. Miners were likely to have a lot of respect for a woman like that. They wouldn't want her to get hurt. And the mayor would make damn sure his sheriff didn't do anything that might risk her life. Besides, from what Nolan had said, the sheriff was sweet on the woman. Cady could make that work in his favor.

So it was going to be all right, Cady told himself. It had to be. Hell, for all he knew, his boys had taken care of the damn sheriff and all the hostages back there, and everything was fine. If that was the case, then he'd move back to the saloon. If the sheriff had come out on top, well, Cady would deal with that when he had to. He figured to be dealing from a position of strength, what with a couple of the town's leading citizens helping him out and the woman where he could hurt her if he had to.

The town wouldn't like it that Nolan and Taylor were going along with him, but he'd let the miners worry about that after he was gone. What happened to them then wasn't any of his business.

He wondered about Boone. He should have told Boone he was leaving, but he hadn't wanted to interrupt him while he was having his fun with the whore. It wouldn't have been polite. Besides, Boone could do more good there at the saloon than anywhere else.

It was all very clear to Cady, though he hoped he wouldn't have to explain it to Boone later. Boone might not see things quite the way Cady did.

He gave Jewel's arm a jerk, just to keep her off balance and to make sure she didn't try to get away. She hadn't said a word since they'd left the Bad Dog, and she didn't say anything now. She just looked at him like he was some kind of horse turd she'd stepped in. Well, she'd change her tune about that later on, after he'd shown her a good time, which he certainly planned on doing. It would be his way of getting back at the half-breed sheriff.

"How much farther is it?" he asked Jesse Nolan.

"Not far. Right up there."

Cady could see the shadowy outlines of a mining shack and the dark hint of a hole in the mountainside.

"Let's get on up there, then," he said. "I'm getting tired of dragging this woman along."

He tightened his grip on her wrist to let her know that he wasn't really getting tired at all. He held his pistol ready in his other hand, just in case either of the miners changed his mind or the woman somehow got away from him.

He didn't want to kill her, but he would if he had to. There was no real reason not to now, except that he had other plans for her. If he had to kill her it wouldn't make much difference, since there was no one around to know until it was too late.

He'd just tell the mayor and that damn sheriff that she was alive. There wasn't any way for them to find out different.

The inside of the mining shack wasn't much to look at in the flickering light of the lamp Nolan lit. It was mostly taken up with Nolan's business office, but there was a cot in a room in back. There was a window, but it was too small for anyone to climb through. Cady shoved Jewel in there and shut the door.

"Now, then," he said to Taylor and Nolan. "Here's the way it's gonna be. You'll tell your men to keep right on working for another day. Then they can start loading the ore onto a wagon. I'm getting a little bored with this place, and it's about time for me to leave. If everything works out, you don't have to worry about a thing."

Taylor and Nolan looked at each other. Some kind of unspoken message must have passed between them, because when they looked back at Cady, they both nodded.

"Good," he said. "Here's another thing. If that sheriff comes up here, I'm not gonna be responsible for what happens to you two. I'd just as soon kill you as not. I don't have a hell of a lot to lose. And I'll kill the woman, too."

"We understand that," Nolan said.

He was a short man with a big nose and bushy eyebrows. He'd waited for a long time to strike it rich, and now that he had he didn't want it to slip away from him.

"How about you?" Cady asked Taylor.

"Me too," Taylor said.

He was taller than Nolan but almost the same age. He'd

had a hard road for more years than he liked to count. He wasn't going to throw his newfound wealth away now. There'd be plenty left after Cady was long gone.

"Good," Cady said. "We have that all settled. Which one of you wants to go back to the saloon and see how things turned out there?"

The two men looked at each other again.

"I'll go," Nolan said.

"Fine. You be back here in thirty minutes, or I'll put a bullet in your buddy's liver."

"They might not care."

"I don't know about them, but I damn sure don't care. You going or not?"

"I'm going. What if your men are still in charge?"

"Tell them what the deal is and let them know I'm staying here. I think I could get to like it."

"All right." Nolan turned to go.

"One other thing," Cady said.

Nolan turned back. "What's that?"

"Bring me some whiskey. I could use a drink."

It was Alky who saw Nolan coming. He went inside to let Mitch know.

"What you reckon he wants?" Alky asked.

Mitch didn't know. He was more concerned with moving the dead bodies out of the saloon. Several of the townspeople who'd heard the shooting had shown up, and they were helping.

Neely and Riley hadn't come back. They were still out looking for Boone.

Rainbow and Fanny Belle had gone back to Fanny Belle's tent, and Ellie West was sitting at a table with

Reid, who was talking to her in low tones. Mitch didn't know what they were talking about, but he figured it wasn't any of his business.

He stepped outside the saloon to talk to Nolan.

"Howdy, sheriff," Nolan said.

He took off his hat and twisted it as if he'd come to the back door of the jail to ask for a handout.

"Nolan," Mitch said. "Looks like we've got us a hell of a mess here."

"You cleaned out Cady's men, did you?"

"Looks like we did."

"I kinda figured you would. Cady ain't never gone up against anybody quite like you before."

Mitch didn't have a comment on that. He said, "You and Taylor doing all right?"

"We're fine. Look, Sheriff, I don't want you to think we wanted anything to happen to you or anybody else."

"I have a pretty good idea what you thought," Mitch said. His voice was flat. "You were just trying to save your skin. I can understand that. But if anything happens to Jewel, I'm holding you responsible, you and Taylor. Hell won't be big enough for you to hide in."

Nolan looked stricken. "Nothing's gonna happen to her, Sheriff. Cady just wants the gold. Then he'll go away peaceably. That's what he said."

What did you expect him to say? Mitch wondered. He said, "He'd better mean it."

"I'm sure he does. You can see how it is, can't you? Me and Sam couldn't risk losing everything, not after we'd worked so hard for it."

Mitch didn't understand at all, but maybe that was because he'd never had anything to lose. He'd worked hard for most of his life, but he'd just never accumulated much. And what he did accumulate seemed to slip right through his fingers.

He said, "You did what you thought you had to do. But because of you, Cady's still on the loose, and he's still got a hold on this town. If you'd kept quiet, he wouldn't."

"You don't know that. He might've killed us. He might have killed Miss Jewel."

Nolan was right about that, but Mitch didn't want to think about it.

"I don't have any fight with you," he said. "What did you come down here to tell me?"

"Nothing. I was just supposed to see how things turned out. And Cady wants a bottle of whiskey."

Mitch laughed. "People in hell want ice water. You can tell him I said that."

"He won't like it."

"I didn't expect him to. And you can tell him something else for me."

Nolan waited.

"Tell him I'm coming for him," Mitch said. "Maybe not now, but soon."

"I'll tell him."

"And he'll never see me when I do."

"I expect he knows that," Nolan said.

Mitch watched as the miner walked back up the road toward his claim. He didn't really blame Nolan and Taylor for what they'd done. They weren't used to dealing with men like Cady. For that matter, neither was Mitch.

But he was going to deal with him. And it wouldn't be long before he did.

Chapter Eighteen

Neely and Riley had figured it would be easy to find a man without any britches on, but they were wrong.

They'd searched every building and outhouse around, but now it was getting on toward morning and there was no sign of Gil Boone. He'd disappeared completely. It was as if he'd never come to Paxton in the first place, which they figured would have been better for all concerned.

"I'll bet the son of a bitch is at least cold," Neely said. "Bare-assed like that."

"I hope he's cold," Riley said. "I damn sure am."

"We might as well give up," Neely said. "Wherever he is, he's got us whipped. Let's go back and tell Mitch we can't find the bastard."

"You reckon he left town?"

"I never thought about that, him with no britches and all. But he might have. And that reminds me. Somebody better go down the road and bring in that fella Cady has down there. We wouldn't want him to ride in and cause trouble in the morning."

"I'll go," Riley said.

Neely said, "You got a lot of coffins to build."

"To hell with that. We can just dump Cady's men in the ground and bury them in their clothes. They don't deserve any better."

"I guess you're right. If you want to go fetch that fella, you go on. I'll tell Mitch."

"Good enough. I don't think he'll give me any trouble."

"He's probably asleep," Neely said. "I would be."

Gil Boone knew he couldn't stay under the saloon much longer. If he was still there when it got light, someone was bound to see him slip out, even though he'd be in the alley. It sounded like half the town was walking around over his head now, and the whole place was going to be crawling with folks when people woke up and found out what had happened.

Boone didn't think of himself as cowardly for what he'd done, leaving the saloon like that. Instead, he thought of himself as sensible. When he'd heard the blast that blew open the back door of the Bad Dog, his hand had gone right for the gun that was in the gunbelt hanging from the bedpost. If that wasn't brave, he didn't know what was.

But before he'd even pulled it from the holster, more shooting had started. Not pistols, though.

Rifles.

That was when he knew that something had gone wrong with Cady's plan. It hadn't taken him long to decide he didn't need to be a part of whatever was happening. So he went out the window and under the building.

It was a good thing he'd hidden there, because it wasn't long before they were out hunting him. He was sure they'd look in all the usual places, but they'd never think that he'd be right there, right under their feet. It was the safest place in town.

But he couldn't stay there forever, and now it was time for him to move out. Like a frightened turtle, he stuck his head out from under the saloon and looked up and down the alley. There was no one in sight, so he came out all the way.

He knew he must look ridiculous, wearing only a shirt and holding a pistol in his right hand. He had to get some clothes, and he had to get them fast. It was going to be daylight before too long.

But where was he going to get anything?

He could chance breaking into a store, or into some-one's house, but that was a little too risky. There was always the chance some man might have a gun handy.

Then he heard voices in the saloon. Someone was coming toward the back door. Boone didn't wait to see who it was. He dropped down and scooted under the building again.

Fanny Belle and Rainbow came into the alley through the wide-open door that was barely hanging on its hinges.

"Red's gonna have to fix that up quick," Rainbow said. "Else he'll have people sneaking out without paying their bar bills."

"I don't think he'll mind," Fanny Belle said. "He's just glad we cleaned his place out for him."

"I was never so glad to hear anything as I was to hear

your voice," Rainbow said. "I thought those bastards were going to kill all of us."

"Not if I could help it. Let's go back to my place and get you something to eat. I could use a drink."

"Me, too," Rainbow said.

"It's too early for you."

"What about you?"

"It's never too early for me," Fanny Belle said.

When they were gone, Boone slid out into the alley. He knew where he was going now.

To the whore's tent.

He'd never known a whorehouse yet that didn't have a few men's clothes lying around in one place or another. He'd wait out back until the older one had gotten a few drinks in her, and then he'd go in. They wouldn't give him any trouble.

Getting there was the trouble, but he managed to do it without being seen. It was awkward as hell, without britches, even sticking to the alleys. The breeze blowing between his legs and his ying-yang flopping made him feel almost completely defenseless. It was a sensation he'd never experienced before, and he didn't like it worth a damn.

He stood outside the back of the tent and listened. He couldn't hear anything from inside, but he knew they were in there. He pushed aside a flap and entered.

The tent was big, and it was partitioned into sections where the business was done. Boone knew that there were other sections, too, like wherever it was that Fanny Belle did her drinking. He stood quietly, listening.

He heard muffled voices near the front of the tent.

Looking behind a partition, he pulled a sheet off a bed and held it in front of him. Walking a little awkwardly, he went off toward the front.

"I don't see how you can drink so much," Rainbow said. She was sitting across the table from Fanny Belle, watching her with an expression that mixed admiration and anxiety. "I'm surprised it doesn't make you sick."

"It works the opposite on me," Fanny Belle said. She drank a big swallow from her glass. "Let me tell you something, honey. After you've been in this business as long as I have, you need something to settle your nerves."

Rainbow said, "I could use a drink, but I hope I don't get to that point."

"So do I, honey. I've been thinking about retiring. This place has been bringing in plenty, and I have a couple of nice bank accounts out in California. You ever give any thought to living in California?"

"I've never been there."

"It's got a nice climate. You'd like it."

"I don't have as much money as you. In fact, I don't have hardly any at all."

"You won't have to worry about that," Fanny Belle assured her.

"And you won't, either, if you mess with me," Boone said, stepping up behind her and putting the barrel of his pistol to her head. "Don't either one of you move."

Fanny Belle's eyes went to the shotgun, which she'd leaned against the tent wall. It was six feet away. It might as well have been six miles.

Rainbow was looking at the front of the sheet. "You don't look quite as big as you did last night."

"Shut your damn mouth, whore. Get up real slow and find me some britches, or I'll put a hole in this old bitch's head. Move it now."

Rainbow stood up slowly. "I don't think there's anything around here that'd quite fit you."

"I don't give a damn about how they fit. And get me a pair of boots while you're at it."

"All right."

"If you come back here with a gun, I'll kill this one before you can do a thing."

"How about if I just shoot you from behind?"

"You could try that," Boone admitted. "I'm betting I'll still have time to pull this trigger before I fall. If you want to try it, go ahead."

"Maybe I will," Rainbow said.

She went out and left them there. Fanny Belle drained her glass and reached out calmly to pour another drink.

"That's enough of that," Boone said.

"That's what you think," Fanny Belle said. "You want some?"

Boone jabbed the pistol into the back of her head hard enough to snap it forward.

"I was just asking," Fanny Belle said.

Rainbow came back, carrying a pair of boots and a pair of worn denim pants.

"You can try these," she said.

Boone realized then that he was going to have a hell of a time getting dressed with one hand while he kept the pistol on Fanny Belle.

"Put them on the table and back off," he said.

Rainbow put the boots and pants on the table and took a step backward. She started fiddling with her hair.

"Back off some more," Boone said, dropping the sheet and swinging the pistol toward her.

That was what Rainbow had been waiting for. Her hand came from behind her head quickly as a striking rattler. With all her strength, she jammed the hatpin hard into that part of Boone where she thought it would do the most good.

The pistol went off, but the bullet missed Rainbow by inches, and Boone didn't get off another shot.

Rainbow would never have guessed a man could scream that loud.

Chapter Nineteen

"We couldn't find him," Neely told Mitch. "Riley's gone down the road to bring in the one that's standing guard down there."

Mitch had forgotten about that little detail. He was too worried about Jewel to think straight.

"Thanks," he told Neely. "Where do you think Boone got to?"

"Don't know. He might have taken off over the mountain. Wherever he is, he's hid good. But he won't get far without clothes."

"He might be looking for clothes, then. Did you check the stores?"

"Yep."

"He might be up at the mine shack with Cady by now. We'll worry about him later. You want to help here?"

"Sure," Neely said.

"Good." Mitch pointed across the room. "You can help Alky get that one over to the jail."

The saloon looked like a war hospital. Seven of Cady's men were dead, and they'd been pulled over to the side of the room. The others, the three of them who could walk, were about to be moved to the jail. The fourth was going to have to stay where he was. Mitch didn't expect him to live much longer. He'd lost too much blood, and there was nothing they could do about that.

"When I come back, we'll go after Cady," Alky said as he came up to them.

"We'll see," Mitch told him.

He looked over at Reid, who beckoned for him to come over to where he was still sitting with Ellie West. Mitch figured he was going to have to talk to Reid sooner or later. Might as well get it over with.

When Mitch approached the table, Ellie West got up and left with a parting smile for Reid.

"I have to get over to the Eat Here and start cooking," she said. "Those miners get hungry for their breakfast whether I've been up all night or not."

"I appreciate what you did," Reid told her. "I figured we'd all die right here."

"The sheriff wasn't going to let that happen," Ellie said.

Reid gave Mitch a sour look. "Didn't do my daughter much good, though."

"I'm leaving now," Ellie said. "Be careful what you say, Pax."

Mitch hid a grin. He'd never heard anyone call Reid that before.

"Sit down," Reid said to Mitch. He waited until Ellie was out of earshot. "I'll say what I damn well please."

"You're the boss," Mitch said.

"Damn right I am. And don't you forget it."

"You're not likely to let me."

Reid started to say something, shook his head, and started over. "Hell, we're getting off on the wrong foot here. You know as well as I do that if your and your little army hadn't come in here shooting the place up like Custer's cavalry, that son of a bitch Cady would have killed me sooner or later. Jewel, too, and all the rest. But it's eating at me that he still has my daughter. You know he's going to kill her, or worse."

"Not if I can help it."

"Yeah. But what can you do?"

"I don't know. He's got her up in Nolan's shack. I plan on going up there to see if there's any way to get at him."

"I'm going with you, then," Reid said.

"No," Mitch said. "I don't want that, and you don't either."

"You just said that I was the boss. I still am. Nothing's changed."

"What's changed is that you're too upset by this. You'd make a mistake."

"You're telling me you're not upset?"

"I'm just telling you I'm less likely to make a mistake."

Reed gave him a level stare. Then his eyes dropped to the table, where his hands were fumbling two poker chips.

"You could be right," Reid said. "But I'm not much good at sitting and waiting."

"Maybe you should go have breakfast."

"That might not be a bad idea." Reid stood up. "I know you don't much like me. You think I tricked you into taking this job in the first place, and maybe I did, at that. But I'm trusting you on this, trusting you with my daughter's life."

"I understand that," Mitch said. "I'll do what I can."

"You'd better," Reid said. "And speaking of trust, what about Bill Carson? I trusted him once, and it didn't work out."

"I'm not Carson," Mitch said.

"Did you catch up to him?" Reid asked.

Mitch nodded.

"But you didn't bring Carson."

"No." Mitch wasn't going to tell Reid what had happened to Carson. Let him think what he wanted to. "But I have the money for you. All of it. You don't have to worry about that."

"I'm not worried about it. The money doesn't mean a thing now. Not until I know that Jewel's safe."

"I said I'll do what I can."

Reid tossed the poker chips into the middle of the table. "Now can you see why I didn't want you to leave town?"

Mitch almost smiled. "It wasn't because you thought somebody like Cady was going to come along and take over. You didn't want me to leave because you were afraid I might not come back. You thought I might just take your money and keep right on going."

"I didn't think that. I trusted you."

"And here I am, right back in the middle of another mess."

"Yeah," Reid said. "I guess when you took this job, you didn't have any idea how much fun it would be."

"You got that right," Mitch said.

* * *

"Goddamn it," Cady said when Nolan came back to the shack and told him what he'd learned at the saloon. "You mean to tell me they killed all of them?"

"Maybe not all," Nolan said. "I couldn't tell. But I doubt anybody's in much shape to do you any good."

"What about Boone?"

"Don't know about him. I didn't see him, though."

Maybe Boone got away, Cady thought. That might give Cady an edge later on if he needed one. And it looked like he might need one. He never thought those townies would have the nerve to stand up to him. It was all that damn sheriff's fault.

"I thought I told you to bring some whiskey," he told Nolan.

"They wouldn't give me any," Nolan said. "They didn't seem real interested in your welfare, to tell you the truth."

"Bastards," Cady said, wishing he could do something to strike back. He thought about Jewel. "I oughta go in there and cut that woman's face. That'd show that mayor who's the boss."

"Before you do, I gotta tell you one other thing."

Cady wasn't much interested in listening to Nolan any longer, but he said, "What's that?"

"The sheriff said to tell you he was coming after you. He said you'd never see him coming, though."

"That's just about what I'd expect some sneaking half-breed to say. He doesn't bother me."

Cady had expected all along that Mitch would come after him. After all, Cady had the mayor's daughter, and the way Nolan had explained things, Reid had the sheriff under his thumb. But Cady figured that as long as he had the woman, the sheriff was pretty much helpless.

Cady was holding another ace as well, or rather two of them: Nolan and Taylor. They didn't know it yet, but they were going to defend him against the sheriff if it came to that.

And there was always Boone. For all Cady knew, Boone was out there causing problems for the sheriff right now.

Cady certainly hoped so.

Gil Boone wasn't causing problems for anyone. He was lying on the floor of Fanny Belle's tent, clutching himself and moaning.

At least he's stopped screaming, Rainbow thought. She'd almost felt sorry for him at first, but Fanny Belle told her she was wasting her sympathy.

"You did the right thing," Fanny Belle said. "That son of a bitch needed something stuck in him a long time ago. I hope he gets the gangrene and the damn thing rots off."

Boone heard her and moaned louder.

"You hush your mouth," Fanny Belle said, bending down to look at him. "I'm going to pull that pin out of you now. Try not to yell so loud."

Boone looked at her with wide eyes. Rainbow was standing over him with the shotgun pointed at his head, but his head was the least of his worries at the moment.

"Here we go, then," Fanny Belle said.

She grabbed the pin and gave a yank. It came out smoothly. Boone closed his eyes and passed out.

"He's not so tough, is he?" Fanny Belle said. She tossed the pin on the table. "What you think we oughta do with him?"

"Take him to the sheriff, I guess," Rainbow said. "But he'll have to get up. I'm not going to carry him."

"Doesn't look like he wants to get up."

"Well," Rainbow said, "we can't just leave him lying there."

Fanny Belle reached out a foot and gave Boone a not-so-gentle nudge, right where the pin had been stuck. Boone's eyes popped open.

"Arrrrrrrr," he said.

"Same to you," Fanny Belle said. "Get on your damn feet."

Boone just looked at her.

"Kick him again," Rainbow said. "Harder this time."

Fanny Belle smiled. "My pleasure."

"No!" Boone said, in what was very nearly a shriek.

"Get on your feet, then," Fanny Belle said.

Boone didn't get up. Instead, he drew himself into a ball so that Fanny Belle couldn't kick him in his private parts.

"Hell," Fanny Belle said. "The sheriff don't care one way or the other about this son of a bitch. Shoot him, Rainbow."

Rainbow looked hesitant. "If you say so."

"Hell, no use for you to do it. Give me that shotgun."

Rainbow handed it over, but by the time Fanny Belle had it, Boone had struggled to his feet.

"At least give me some britches," he said.

"Forget the britches," Fanny Belle told him. "Start walking."

After a second or two, he did.

Chapter Twenty

It was just getting to be full daylight. Alky was on his way back to the saloon when he saw Fanny Belle, Rainbow, and Gil Boone coming down the street. People all along the way were stopped, their mouths hanging open at the sight.

"Rounding up customers?" Alky asked Fanny Belle when they drew back even with him.

"Just returning one in damaged condition," Fanny Belle said. "You want him?"

Alky thought it over. "Sheriff might want to see him first. I don't think he'd want to miss a sight like this."

Boone glared at him, but it wasn't a very effective glare, considering his situation.

"Come on," Alky said, leading the way.

They were almost to the saloon when Evan Riley came riding up the road on Frank Deevers's horse and leading Deevers along behind. Deevers's hands were tied behind his back, and there was a rope around his neck. About every third step, Deevers stumbled, but he didn't fall, and Riley didn't seem to notice.

Riley pulled back on the reins and stopped the horse in the middle of the street, watching the little procession.

"If that don't beat everything," he said. He turned in the saddle and addressed Deevers. "Looks like one of your pards got himself in a real mess."

Deevers was watching too. "Boone?" he said. "Is that Boone?"

"Sure looks like him," Riley said. "Not that I know him all that well."

They watched as Boone was ushered into the saloon. Riley couldn't get the grin off his face.

"I was gonna take you to the jail," he told Deevers. "But I think we oughta stop here and see what happens."

"Just take me to the damn jail," Deevers said. "I've seen all I want to see."

When he saw Boone, Mitch grinned. When Fanny Belle told how she and Rainbow had captured him, everyone in the saloon laughed, except for Deevers, whom Riley had refused to take to the jail. Even Reid laughed, though not much and not long.

"Alky," Mitch said after the story was told, "take the prisoner to the jail. And find him some pants while you're at it."

"I think his pants are in the back room," Rainbow said. "Where he left them."

There was more laughter at that, and Alky went in search of the pants. Riley introduced Deevers to the crowd and explained that he'd been sleeping at his post.

"Made my job pretty simple," Riley said. "Want him to go to the jail, Sheriff?"

"You and Alky can take him and Boone on over," Mitch said. "I've got a job that needs finishing."

"Need any help?" Riley asked.

"Thanks," Mitch said. "But I'll do better on my own."

Cady had made up his mind what he was going to do. He'd take the woman along with him in the gold wagon and drive down the mountain. If they followed him, he'd kill her.

They might get him if he did, and they might get the gold, but they'd always know they'd been the cause of her death.

Of course, if they didn't follow him, he'd kill her anyway. What the hell else could he do with her? But they didn't know that. He'd tell them that he'd let her go somewhere on the trail, and they'd have to believe him. What choice did they have?

He'd take Nolan and Taylor along, too. They could watch his back. If they gave him any trouble, hell, he'd shoot them. And when he killed the woman, he'd kill them. It wouldn't be hard to get the drop on them.

They could have their men finish loading the wagon that night, and they'd pull out the next morning. Cady didn't want to leave at night. That would be giving the half-breed sheriff too good a chance to follow him.

So all he had to do was get through one more day and one more night. He didn't think the sheriff would try anything during the daylight. There wasn't any way he could sneak up on the shack without being seen.

Cady called Taylor and Nolan and said, "I want the two of you to keep a watch for me. I need some sleep, so I'll have to trust you to wake me if there's trouble. I'll be in the back room with the woman, and if anything happens, she's going to be the first one to die. You understand that?"

Taylor and Nolan said that they understood.

"And you'll be the next. You understand that, too?"

They nodded.

Cady knew what they were thinking. They were thinking that as soon as he got to sleep, they'd get away.

Or maybe they thought they could get into the room and capture him. Maybe they even thought they could kill him.

Well, maybe they could, if he was asleep. But he wasn't going to be asleep. No need to tell them that, though. Let them find out the hard way.

"Another day or so, and everything's gonna be just fine," he said. "You can go back to your mining, and things will be just like they were before."

Nolan and Taylor weren't stupid. They knew things would never be like they were before. They'd put saving their own skins, not to mention their mines, above everything. It would be a long time before the town forgave them for that, if it ever did. But there was no use in trying to say any of that to Cady. So they just tried to smile and pretend they believed him.

"What do you think?" Taylor asked when Cady had shut himself in the room with Jewel.

"I think he's not about to go to sleep," Nolan said. "He's gonna molest Reid's daughter, is what he's gonna do."

"She might have something to say about that," Taylor said.

"Yeah," Nolan said. "But he's the one with the gun."

Jewel watched Cady close the door. He turned to her and smiled what he probably thought was an engaging smile.

It didn't engage Jewel. To her, Cady looked predatory and cruel, like some kind of wild animal that had on a human skin for a while.

"I think it's about time we got to know each other," Cady said.

Jewel just looked at him. She wasn't going to say anything unless she had to.

"You're a fine-looking woman," he said.

Jewel didn't respond.

"You might as well talk to me," Cady said. He showed her the pistol in his right hand. "I'd hate to have to use this on you, but I would if I had to."

"No, you wouldn't," Jewel said. "Then you wouldn't have any advantage."

"I'd have those two outside."

"I don't think anyone cares much about them anymore," Jewel said. "People don't like turncoats."

Cady laughed. "Nobody's gonna want to make me kill them, though. And I'd hate to have to kill you. But I'd do it if I had to."

"I know you would."

"That's just business. It doesn't mean we can't have a little fun together."

Jewel wondered what chance she had to get her hands on his gun. None, the way things stood. Maybe if he were relaxed and off guard, the odds would shift a little.

"I guess you're not the worst-looking man I ever saw," she said.

Cady gave her a smile that was no more engaging than his first had been. "I thought I'd start looking better to you after you thought things over a little."

The only furniture in the room was a small cot, and

Jewel was already sitting on it. Cady walked over and stood by her.

"Why don't you make some room for me on that thing," he said.

Jewel scooted slightly to her left, and Cady sat down beside her. He put his arm around her, but he didn't let go of the gun. Jewel could smell whiskey on his breath and in his clothes.

"I know a lot of women that would give a pretty penny to be where you are right now," Cady said.

Jewel couldn't think of a single one. She doubted that Cady could, either. She let him put his arm around her, and she didn't cringe much when he leaned over to plant a kiss on her cheek.

Just lead him on, she told herself. *Let him believe he's getting somewhere, and then maybe I can get my hands on that gun.*

Cady got up and put the gun on the far side of the room, out of reach. It was almost as if he had known what she was thinking.

"Now," he said, unbuckling his belt, "we can have ourselves a little fun."

Things hadn't proceeded at all as Jewel had hoped. Cady wasn't going to let down his guard after all.

"Don't touch me," she said.

"Oh, I'll touch you, all right," Cady said.

He stepped over to her and threw a short right that took her on the point of the chin and snapped her head back. She fell back, her head striking the wall. Her body relaxed, and she slumped on the cot.

Cady smiled and took off his boots and pants.

Chapter Twenty-one

Mitch looked over an outcropping of rock and scanned the area around the mine shack. Nolan's operation wasn't as big as Reid's, but it had a stamping mill, silent now in the early morning, and a couple of small sheds. There was a corral where the mules that hauled the wagons were kept, not far from the opening of the mine itself. Near the corral was a wagon with a canvas sheet tied over it. The mine shaft was sunk into the mountain face, and a cart track ran down into it.

The mining shack sat on the side of the mountain, well away from the open mouth of the mine and the stamping mill. There were no trees anywhere around, and there was no way to come up to the shack without being seen, though the stamping mill would provide cover for some of the distance. Mitch knew Cady was in the shack watching for him right now. Or if not Cady, Taylor or

Nolan. If Mitch were to stick his head over the rock any farther, one of them might take a shot at him.

The early-morning sun warmed the mountainside, and Mitch could feel the warmth soaking into his body. He'd have liked to be somewhere asleep in a big feather bed right about now, but he knew he'd never sleep well again if he didn't get Jewel away from Cady.

Mitch no longer cared what happened to either Taylor or Nolan. They'd backed a losing hand when they decided to go over to Cady, and they'd have to live or die with that decision. He didn't want to have to kill either one of them, but if they got in his way, he would. He figured that Cady would do the same.

He looked back down the road toward town. It wouldn't be long before Nolan's men came to work the mine, to get the last of the gold that Cady planned to haul out of town. How he thought he could get away with it, Mitch didn't know.

Before he'd left town, he'd had a little talk with Alky. He'd told him where to hide and what to do. Alky hadn't been too sure about it.

"I'm not the shot you are," he'd told Mitch. "Maybe you better do it."

"If anybody has to shoot Cady while he's leaving town, I'll already be dead," Mitch said. "This is a plan of last resort."

"What if he has Miss Jewel with him?"

"He probably will. But you're going to kill him before he has a chance to hurt her."

"I'm not so sure," Alky said.

"But you'll try."

Alky had thought it over. "I guess I will if I have to. Damn. I hope you come walking back down that road before too long."

"So do I," Mitch said.

He still hoped so, but he couldn't figure out how he was going to get inside that shack without just charging it head-on. And if he did that, he had about one chance in a million of getting to the door before he got shot.

He thought about that for a minute, and then he saw a couple of the miners coming up the road. He realized they would have to pass within a few yards of the stamping mill on their way to the mine. That was his answer.

He slipped down behind the rock and started back toward town.

Jewel shook her head to clear it and looked at Cady. He smiled at her, and she rolled off the cot, hitting the floor and spinning toward the pistol.

Cady stopped smiling. He had his pants half off, but he jumped for her anyway. His heel caught in a pants leg, and he went sprawling.

Jewel came up with the pistol and saw Cady crawling toward her. She cocked the hammer and was about to pull the trigger when he lunged. His arm struck her hand, sending the pistol barrel toward the ceiling as Jewel tried to fire the gun.

Cady lunged for the gun, but Jewel jerked her arm aside. Then she swung it back, striking Cady in the side of the head with the barrel.

He fell to the side, and Jewel tried to get to her feet.

She almost made it, but Cady reached out, grabbed her ankle, and yanked it toward him.

Jewel fell hard and lost her grip on the pistol. Cady scrabbled over her and picked it up. He pushed himself over by the cot and sat there panting.

Jewel looked at him, wondering when she'd get another chance at the pistol. Cady didn't look like he'd ever let it go again, but she never doubted that he would.

"Reckon we ought to go in there?" Nolan asked Taylor when the first sounds of the struggle reached them.

"Not any of our business. We're supposed to sit out here and watch."

Nolan wished he could be as hard-minded about things as Taylor. It ate at him to think what might be happening to Jewel, though. He knew it was wrong to let it happen, but he was too afraid of what might happen to *him* to interrupt Cady. What if Cady took a shot at him? Where would he be then?

So he didn't do a thing except look out the window and watch his men coming to work. He didn't turn around, not even when he heard the scuffling in the room behind him.

But because he was looking down the road and watching for the wrong thing, for Mitch Frye, he missed seeing what he was looking for.

One of the men who went inside the stamping mill wasn't one of Nolan's hands. It was Mitch. He didn't waste any time inside, where the rock from the mine was broken down into the ore that Cady planned to haul away. He didn't care about the machinery or the men who were getting ready to operate it. He just cared about Jewel.

So he walked right on through the mill, up two sets of stairs, and out the back door. He slipped down behind the mine shack and crouched under the small back window, listening.

Mitch could hear the sounds of a scuffle, but the back window was too small to admit him. He'd have to go in through the front, where he knew someone would be watching.

To get their attention, he fired two shots through the upper back wall of the shack, counted to three, and ran to the front.

He got up almost to the porch before the door burst open. Jesse Taylor was standing there with a pistol in his hand. He hadn't been fooled by Mitch's attempt at a diversion.

"You stop right there, Sheriff," he said.

Mitch didn't stop. He shot Taylor in the shoulder. Taylor yelled and fell to the porch, then rolled off. Mitch went past him without a glance and entered the shack.

Nolan was there, holding his hands up with the palms facing outward.

"I'm not going to try to stop you," he said. "You don't have to shoot me. Cady's in the back room."

Mitch took a step forward just as the door to the room came open. Jewel was standing there, a pained look on her face. Cady was right behind her, twisting her left arm up behind her back. His pistol was against the back of her head.

"You do have a way of messing up my plans," he told Mitch. "Who the hell are you, anyhow?"

"I'm the sheriff."

"Hell, I know that. Now get out of my way."

Mitch didn't move until Cady gave an upward yank on Jewel's arm. She grimaced but didn't cry out.

"I said get out of the way," Cady told Mitch. "I'll jerk her damn arm off if you don't."

Mitch stepped back.

"Get on out of here," Cady said. "All the way out. And Nolan, you come with me. We'll just take whatever your boys have loaded on that wagon already and clear out."

Mitch went outside and waited until Cady, Nolan, and Jewel had come out as well.

"Shoot him, Mitch," Jewel said.

"Mitch," Cady said. "Funny name for a half-breed. You know better than to try anything, don't you?"

Mitch said that he did. He might be able to kill Cady before he put a shot into Jewel's head, but he might not. He couldn't take the chance.

"Put your pistol down on the ground," Cady said. "Now."

Mitch obeyed, laying the pistol down carefully. He straightened up and looked at Cady.

"We're just gonna walk over by the mine and get on that wagon there," Cady said. "Then we'll leave you and your little town alone."

Mitch had noticed the wagon earlier, but he hadn't thought anything about it. Now he wished he'd paid it a little more attention.

Some of the miners were standing at the opening in the

mountain, looking back toward the shack. Mitch wondered if they'd be of any help.

"Tell one of them to hitch the mules to that wagon," Cady said.

Nolan walked up toward the mine and yelled at the men. They stood for a minute, talking among themselves, and then all but one of them went inside. The one who was left went over to a little corral where four mules were standing around doing nothing.

"Let's go," Cady said, half dragging Jewel along over the rough ground.

They were about halfway there when Jewel seemed to turn her ankle on a rock. She sagged back against Cady. Cady faltered, and Jewel swung her right elbow into his stomach. He released his hold on her arm, and she jumped to one side, falling to the ground.

Mitch had already picked up his gun by that time, and he snapped off a shot at Cady, who fired back and started running up the steep trail to the corral.

The man in the corral looked up at the commotion. Cady shot him, ran through the gate, grabbed the mule's skimpy mane in one hand, and pulled himself up. He kicked his heels into its side. The mule lurched forward, then broke into a run.

Cady began firing his pistol as soon as the mule cleared the gate. He shot Nolan, who fell near Jewel. He tried for Jewel, but the bullet sang off a nearby rock. And he tried for Mitch, but by that time he was bouncing too much on the mule for any kind of accuracy.

Cady jerked the mule's head, turning it straight for Mitch, trying to run him down. Mitch shot at him twice and missed both times. It wasn't easy to hit a rider on a running mule, especially when the rider wasn't staying anywhere near still.

Should have shot the damn mule, Mitch thought, but Cady was by him and on his way down the road before Mitch could get off another round.

There was nothing to do except go after him. Mitch ran for the corral, pausing only long enough to see that Jewel was all right. He got on a mule and started after Cady.

Chapter Twenty-two

It was as bumpy a ride as Mitch had ever had, and he figured the mule he was on had the sharpest backbone of any animal God ever made. But it sure could run. It was more surefooted than a horse would have been on the rocks, too.

They tore down the road behind Cady, who was heading straight for the middle of town. Mitch wondered if anyone would try to stop him.

Probably not. No one knew he was coming.

When they reached the town, they flew down the street, scattering several townspeople who were crossing it and a couple of dogs that were trying to sleep in the sun. Mitch saw Alky run out of the jail to see what the ruckus was all about. Too bad Alky wasn't already set up where Mitch had told him to be. He might have had a chance to shoot Cady off the mule, though it was moving a lot faster than a wagon would have been.

They went through the town and on down the mountain. Mitch was beginning to think that Cady stood a good chance of getting away, since Mitch was pretty sure the mule he was riding was going to split him in half before much longer. He didn't even bother to try a shot. He was a good rider, even bareback, but he'd have been lucky to hit the mountain itself.

He saw Cady glance back over his shoulder at him. The son of a bitch was laughing. He must have been pretty sure he was going to get away. Mitch didn't want that to happen, but he didn't know what he could do to stop it.

And then someone shot Cady's mule.

There was the crack of a rifle, and the mule stopped as suddenly and completely as if it had run into a wall. Cady pinwheeled over its ears and hit the road flat on his back in a puff of dust. The mule fell heavily to one side.

Mitch realized that he had a serious problem, one that he hadn't thought of until that moment: How was he going to stop a mule that was plunging headlong down a mountain road without any reins or a bit in its mouth?

He hauled back on the mule's mane, pulling its head high. The mule didn't stop. It didn't even slow down that Mitch could tell.

Cady rolled over onto his side and fired into the trees. Puffs of dust hopped out of the road beside him. Mitch wondered who was doing the shooting, but he didn't have time to think too much about it.

He raced past Cady, who was scrambling toward cover. A couple of feet to the left and the mule would have run right over him, which might have solved all Mitch's problems. But it didn't work out, and Mitch was past Cady and on down the road.

Mitch figured that if he didn't get stopped soon, he'd be at the bottom of the mountain before he did. Or maybe the mule would just keep on running until doomsday. In desperation, Mitch leaned forward and grabbed one of the mule's ears. He pulled it back toward him, and when it was close enough, he bit down on it as hard as he could.

That stopped the mule, all right. Its legs stiffened and locked, and if Mitch hadn't had his arm wrapped tightly around its neck, he'd have hit the ground just as Cady had. As it was, he managed to slide off the mule's back as it stood there and eee-yawed its displeasure.

Mitch ran back up the road, where the sound of shots was still echoing. He figured to come up behind Cady and take him by surprise.

He should have known better. Cady had the survival instincts of a wild animal. Mitch was certain that he hadn't made a sound, but as soon as he got within sight of Cady, the outlaw spun around and fired a shot that ripped the bark off a tree near Mitch's head.

Mitch dived under a bush and rolled. Leaves pattered down as a bullet split a limb just above him.

But Cady was also occupied by the rifleman across the road, whoever it was. Mitch was able to get behind the trunk of a large pine. However, he didn't have a clear shot at Cady. He was going to have to move.

It was easy to do, because the rifleman sent a volley of shots in Cady's direction. None of them hit Cady, but a couple came close enough to Mitch to give him a chill. He'd have to have a talk with the shooter later on.

For the moment, he satisfied himself by crossing an open stretch of ground and getting behind a rock that was out of the line of the rifleman's fire. But when he looked out from his hiding place, Cady was gone.

Cady was angry with himself, with the damn sheriff, with the mule, and with whoever had shot the animal. He'd had a good plan, and it would have made him rich, richer than he'd ever have become in the ordinary way of thievery and killing that he'd practiced for the last several years. But it was all ruined. Now he'd be lucky to get off the damn mountain alive.

Well, the mule was already dead, so Cady couldn't get revenge on it. And Cady wasn't about to kill himself. That still left him two targets, however. First he'd deal with whoever was shooting the rifle, and then he'd get the sheriff.

He came out from behind his rock and crossed the road at a dead run. He didn't bother trying to fire his pistol. There'd be plenty of time for that when he got to the trees on the other side.

A bullet buzzed by his ear, but he just grinned. *Keep on shooting*, he thought. *Let me know right where you are*.

He got to the trees, hit the ground, and did a rolling somersault. When he came up, he had his pistol leveled at a very surprised man who was holding a rifle but who wasn't quite sure where to aim it.

"Drop it, Mr. Mayor," Cady said. "Else I'll have to shoot you where you stand."

Reid hesitated.

Cady fired a shot that came close to clipping Reid's right earlobe.

Reid dropped the rifle.

Cady stood up. "I thought you'd see it my way. Now

you're gonna have to help me get down off this mountain in one piece."

"The hell I will," Reid said.

"Up to you," Cady said. "It's either that, or I kill you."

"You'll kill me anyway."

Cady grinned. "I might, at that. But then again, I might not. You can't be sure. So what're you gonna do?"

Reid didn't answer, which Cady took to mean that he'd do as he was told. "You just move away from the rifle, and I'll pick it up. It might come in handy."

Reid took a couple of steps to the side, and Cady retrieved the rifle. He straightened up and said, "All right, let's take us a little walk. You first."

When they emerged from the trees, Reid was about two paces in front of Cady, who scanned the trees on the other side of the road and looked up and down the mountain. There was no movement, no sound. It was quiet as a graveyard.

"Hey, Sheriff," Cady called. "You out there anywhere?"

There was no answer. Somewhere in the distance a jay screeched.

"Wonder where the son of a bitch went?" Cady said to no one in particular.

He prodded Reid in the back with the rifle, and they started walking. Cady moved to one side of Reid so that Mitch couldn't get a shot at him from the other side of the road.

The dead mule lay just ahead of them. Flies were circling the bloody hole in its head.

"Lucky shot?" Cady asked.

"I was aiming at you," Reid said.

"Figured you were. Too bad you killed that mule,

though. It would've got me off this mountain in another few minutes. If it weren't for bad luck, I wouldn't have any luck at all."

"I should have aimed at the mule," Reid said. "That way I might have hit you."

"Might have, considering the way things have been going for me. At least they can't get much worse."

But he was wrong about that. Mitch stood up from where he'd been lying down beside the dead mule and shot him through the head.

Cady didn't even have time to look surprised. The back of his head blew away, and he fell to the road and lay still.

"I was wondering where you were," Reid said. "Is Jewel all right?"

Mitch looked down at Cady, then back at Reid. "She's fine. What were you doing here? Trying to make sure I didn't leave town again?"

"Goddamn it," Reid said. "I . . . wait a minute. Are you making a joke?"

"Not much of one," Mitch said. "You didn't answer my question."

"I'm here because I talked to Alky, and he told me you weren't sure you'd be able to take Cady and that you wanted him down here to be sure Cady didn't get away. Since I'm the mayor, I told him I'd be the one to see to that job. It was my daughter Cady had, after all."

"You came closer to killing me than you did to killing Cady."

"I stopped him, didn't I?"

"You stopped him, all right," Mitch said. "I'll have to admit that. Shooting the mule was a good idea."

"Yeah," Reid said.

"It's not going to make Nolan very happy, though. It's his mule."

"To hell with Nolan. He and Taylor aren't any better than outlaws themselves. They're finished in Paxton."

"They have their mines. They won't leave."

"We'll see about that."

Mitch didn't feel like arguing. He didn't know about anyone else, but as far as he was concerned, whatever Nolan and Taylor had done was already forgotten. For that matter, Taylor might even be dead. Mitch wasn't sure. Jewel was all right, though. That was all Mitch cared about for the moment.

"Let's go on back to town," he said.

Reid picked up his rifle from where Cady had dropped it when he died. They left Cady and the mule lying in the road and started walking.

MOVING ON
JANE CANDIA COLEMAN

Jane Candia Coleman is a magical storyteller who spins brilliant tales of human survival, hope, and courage on the American frontier, and nowhere is her marvelous talent more in evidence than in this acclaimed collection of her finest work. From a haunting story of the night Billy the Kid died, to a dramatic account of a breathtaking horse race, including two stories that won the prestigious Spur Award, here is a collection that reveals the passion and fortitude of its characters, and also the power of a wonderful writer.

___4545-1 $4.99 US/$5.99 CAN

INCIDENT at BUFFALO CROSSING

ROBERT J. CONLEY

The Sacred Hill. It rose above the land, drawing men to it like a beacon. But the men who came each had their own dreams. There is Zeno Bond, the settler who dreams of land and empire. There is Mat McDonald, captain of the steamship *John Hart*, heading the looming war between the Spanish and the Americans. And there is Walker, the Cherokee warrior called by a vision he cannot deny—a vision of life, death...and destiny.

___4396-3 $4.50 US/$5.50 CAN

Dorchester Publishing Co., Inc.
P.O. Box 6640
Wayne, PA 19087-8640

Please add $1.75 for shipping and handling for the first book and $.50 for each book thereafter. NY, NYC, and PA residents, please add appropriate sales tax. No cash, stamps, or C.O.D.s. All orders shipped within 6 weeks via postal service book rate. Canadian orders require $2.00 extra postage and must be paid in U.S. dollars through a U.S. banking facility.

Name_____
Address_____
City_____ State_____ Zip_____
I have enclosed $_____ in payment for the checked book(s).
Payment <u>must</u> accompany all orders. ☐ Please send a free catalog.
CHECK OUT OUR WEBSITE! www.dorchesterpub.com

THE ACTOR

ROBERT J. CONLEY

Bluford Steele had always been an outsider until he found his calling as an actor. Instead of being just another half-breed Cherokee with a white man's education, he can be whomever he chooses. But when the traveling acting troupe he is with arrives in the wild, lawless town of West Riddle, the man who rules the town with an iron fist forces them to perform. Then he steals all the proceeds. Steele is determined to get the money back, even if it means playing the most dangerous role of his life—a cold-blooded gunslinger ready to face down any man who gets in his way.

___4498-6 $4.50 US/$5.50 CAN

WILDERNESS

#24

Mountain Madness

⟵————————————⟶

David Thompson

When Nate King comes upon a pair of green would-be trappers from New York, he is only too glad to risk his life to save them from a Piegan war party. It is only after he takes them into his own cabin that he realizes they will repay his kindness...with betrayal. When the backshooters reveal their true colors, Nate knows he is in for a brutal battle—with the lives of his family hanging in the balance.

___4399-8 $3.99 US/$4.99 CAN

Dorchester Publishing Co., Inc.
P.O. Box 6640
Wayne, PA 19087-8640

WILDERNESS

#25
FRONTIER MAYHEM

←⟶

David Thompson

The unforgiving wilderness of the Rocky Mountains forces a boy to grow up fast, so Nate King taught his son, Zach, how to survive the constant hazards and hardships—and he taught him well. With an Indian war party on the prowl and a marauding grizzly on the loose, young Zach is about to face the test of his life, with no room for failure. But there is one danger Nate hasn't prepared Zach for—a beautiful girl with blue eyes.

___4433-1 $3.99 US/$4.99 CAN

COTTON SMITH
DARK TRAIL TO DODGE

Tyrel Bannon knows more about a plow than longhorn cattle, but the green farm boy is determined to become a Triple C rider on the long, hard drive from Texas to Dodge, the "Queen City of the Cowtowns." But this is a trail that only the brave, smart and lucky can survive. Waiting ahead are Kiowa warriors, raging rivers, drought, storms . . . and vicious rustlers out to blacken the dust with Triple C blood.

___4510-9 $4.50 US/$5.50 CAN

Dorchester Publishing Co., Inc.
P.O. Box 6640
Wayne, PA 19087-8640

Please add $1.75 for shipping and handling for the first book and $.50 for each book thereafter. NY, NYC, and PA residents, please add appropriate sales tax. No cash, stamps, or C.O.D.s. All orders shipped within 6 weeks via postal service book rate. Canadian orders require $2.00 extra postage and must be paid in U.S. dollars through a U.S. banking facility.

Name_____
Address_____
City_____State_____Zip_____
I have enclosed $_____ in payment for the checked book(s).
Payment <u>must</u> accompany all orders. ❑ Please send a free catalog.
    CHECK OUT OUR WEBSITE! www.dorchesterpub.com

CHEYENNE

BLOODY BONES CANYON/
RENEGADE SIEGE

JUDD COLE

Bloody Bones Canyon. Only Touch the Sky can defend them from the warriors that threaten to take over the camp. But when his people need him most, the mighty shaman is forced to avenge the slaughter of their peace chief. Even Touch the Sky cannot fight two battles at once, and without his powerful magic his people will be doomed.

And in the same action-packed volume . . .

Renegade Siege. Touch the Sky's blood enemies have surrounded a pioneer mining camp and are preparing to sweep down on it like a killing wind. If the mighty shaman cannot hold off the murderous attack, the settlers will be wiped out . . . and Touch the Sky's own camp will be next!

___4586-9 $4.99 US/$5.99 CAN

Dorchester Publishing Co., Inc.
P.O. Box 6640
Wayne, PA 19087-8640

Please add $1.75 for shipping and handling for the first book and $.50 for each book thereafter. NY, NYC, and PA residents, please add appropriate sales tax. No cash, stamps, or C.O.D.s. All orders shipped within 6 weeks via postal service book rate. Canadian orders require $2.00 extra postage and must be paid in U.S. dollars through a U.S. banking facility.

Name_____
Address_____
City_____ State_____ Zip_____
I have enclosed $_____ in payment for the checked book(s).
Payment <u>must</u> accompany all orders. ❏ Please send a free catalog.
CHECK OUT OUR WEBSITE! www.dorchesterpub.com

CHEYENNE

VENGEANCE QUEST/
WARRIOR FURY

JUDD COLE

Vengeance Quest. When his cunning rivals kill a loyal friend in their quest to create a renegade nation, Touch the Sky sets out on a bloody trail that will lead to either revenge on his hated foes—or his own savage death.

And in the same action-packed volume . . .

Warrior Fury. After luring Touch the Sky away from the Cheyenne camp, murderous backshooters dare to kidnap his wife and newborn son. If Touch the Sky fails to save his family, he will kill his foes with his bare hands—then spend eternity walking an endless trail of tears.

___4531-1 $4.99 US/$5.99 CAN

Dorchester Publishing Co., Inc.
P.O. Box 6640
Wayne, PA 19087-8640

CHEYENNE

JUDD COLE

Follow the adventures of Touch the Sky as he searches for a world he can call his own!

#3: Renegade Justice. When his adopted white parents fall victim to a gang of ruthless outlaws, Touch the Sky swears to save them—even if it means losing the trust he has risked his life to win from the Cheyenne.
__3385-2 $3.50 US/$4.50 CAN

#4: Vision Quest. While seeking a mystical sign from the Great Spirit, Touch the Sky is relentlessly pursued by his enemies. But the young brave will battle any peril that stands between him and the vision of his destiny.
__3411-5 $3.50 US/$4.50 CAN

ATTENTION WESTERN CUSTOMERS!

SPECIAL
TOLL-FREE NUMBER
1-800-481-9191

**Call Monday through Friday
10 a.m. to 9 p.m.
Eastern Time
*Get a free catalogue,
join the Western Book Club,
and order books using your
Visa, MasterCard,
or Discover*®.**

*Leisure
Books*